UnBalanced Harmony

A Collection

E. EVANS BUNTIN

Copyright ©2012 E. Evans Buntin
All rights reserved.

ISBN: 0985618205
ISBN-13: 978-0-9856182-0-9

Library of Congress Control Number: 2012915266
Buntella Publication - Poetic Art & Photography
Printed in the United States of America
Antioch, Tennessee

Inside Photos by E. Evans Buntin

For information E-mail: ebuntin3004@gmail.com

This is a work of fiction. Names, characters, places, and incidents either are the product of the author's imagination or are used fictitiously, and any resemblance to actual person, living or dead, business establishment, events, or locales is entirely coincidental.

Without limiting the rights under copyright reserved above, no part of this publication may be reproduced, or stored in or introduced into a retrieval system, or transmitted in any form, or by any means (electronic, mechanical, photocopying, recording, or otherwise), without the prior written permission of the author. Brief passages may be quoted in critical articles and reviews.

ACKNOWLEDGEMENTS

Many thanks to Michael for believing; Dr. Barbara Hodges, whose encouragement, belief and gentle pushes made this publication a reality; my mom, Florence Ella, and my dad, Edmond; Shirley Ann Akins and Teresa Y. Turner, gone too soon; DM Martin, C. Thompson, E. Fletcher, Autumn, Mikey, Antonia, all my friends and family who have encouraged me throughout the years; and this work would not be possible without LillyAnn, Cherri Jubilee, Miranda, Swan, Glacier (please stop talking), and all my characters who came forth and kept insisting...

To Mai Vaughter Manchester, thanks for your contributions – *Metamorphosis* and *Friday's Ritual*.

And to you for taking the time....

To Pat,
Thanks for your support. Good luck in your writing.

Ellen Birth
3/30/13

PART ONE - THE COLLECTION

	Intro - Inside My Head	ix
1	PURE OF HEART	1
	Part I: Frankie Lee's Heart	3
	Part II: Fade to Black	9
	Part III: Pray Until Something Happens	13
	Part IV: LillyAnn's Heart	27
2	QUICK AS A BREATH	
	Part I: Death Plays Inside My Head	35
	Part II: First Born	41
3	In A Bottle	57
4	Society Thin	109
5	Metamorphosis*	117
6	Friday's Ritual*	135

*Metamorphosis and Fridays Ritual by Mai Vaughter Manchester

7	A Life for a Life	137
8	The Barn	147
9	Remembrance	151
10	Popsicle Sticks To My Tongue	157
11	Purple Passion	159
12	If Tomorrow	163
13	Revelation	165
14	A Page From My Diary	173
15	Joe's Life	179
16	Samatha's Night Out	181

PART TWO-POETRY FROM* "LIVING IN THE GARDEN OF REALITY"

Vicious Cycle	187
Words	189
I Am Grown	193
Untitled for a Reason	197
Freedom Came From the Shadowy Mist	199
The Evil Flew Out (her side)	203
Pain of a Fat Kid	207
Touched Death	209
Thinking Man's Blues	211
Final Act	213
Self Loved	215
My Boy	217
The Honor Roll**	219
My Little Brother	221
Angie, My Little Girl***	222
Virgin Seduction	225
Touching the Top	227
Judge Me	229
The Journey	231
Seeing Through Me	233
Sometimes the Silence	235
UnBalanced Harmony (back cover)	

**The Honor Roll (<u>Best Poems of 1995 - The National Library of Poetry</u>)

****A'lice, My Little Girl* - Winner of Editor's Choice Award 1994 (<u>River of Dreams - The National Library of Poetry</u>)

*proposed publication date 2013 - title subject to change

Inside My Head

I've heard them since I can remember, spinning stories in my head. When I was younger I thought I was crazy and did not expose to anyone the voices I heard. No one else spoke of voices that clearly spun a tale every second when their mind was not occupied with normal day to day chores. When I was six, I tried to tell my tales to three fellow first graders only to be reprimanded by my teacher. The trouble I was in, let's just say my ladies were silent to the outside world for far too long. It wasn't until I was in my late twenties that I realized that the voices were only characters waiting for me to put ink to paper and tell their tales.

When I did put pen to paper and finally told the story of each character (for only my review), I found my characters went silent awhile, however, some have been quite stubborn and demanded more time, longer stories. New ones pop up from now to then that I try to vanish to the cobwebs of my minds. Have I given in to letting others read their stories or making their stories a book, no, I sort of like them *inside my head*. I know I'm never alone. I have to watch out and stay within the confines of normal, everyday living, and not let "them" take all my time. I hope this is considered a normal writer's life. My stories are character driven, with each taking the course they want.

Some fifty years since I first heard a voice, I'm now ready to start telling their stories, for fear more than anything that I will die before anyone can meet them.

Meet the ladies *Inside My Head*.

After all, I'm only the storyteller.

PURE
OF
HEART

PART I: FRANKIE LEE'S HEART

As I fall to my knees, I have prayed from the first day of January that Cupid would launch his arrow into Frankie Lee's heart and send to me his Valentine card. Well it's now February 12, only two more days before the god of love influences Frankie Lee.

All of the other girls in Ms. Fabershine's freshman homeroom brag about the boys they've been out on dates with. They're only fourteen, but you should heard the unmentionable things they were doing, especially Margaret Ann. She was holding hands with one boy and even went as far as to let Casey Stevens French kiss her. I wonder how that boy learned how to do that, considering France is way down yonder.

I know because I asked our history teacher, Mr. Myles Age. He told me, "French kissing is something they do in France and it's too far away for you to worry about." Of course, Margaret Ann and Cindy Lee didn't disclose their little dating secrets to me. When I heard the door open, I would flip my legs up and stay pin drop quiet as I eavesdropped from the stall in the bathroom.

But you know, when I ask Papa about going out on a date with a boy, he sent me to my room and told me to come out when I'm thirty. Can you imagine that!

I usually don't take to praying much, but Aunt Ida Mai said you've got to really pray hard if you want something bad enough and if you haven't asked for anything in a long time, then she reckons you're deserving. Besides, all I'm praying for is one little Valentine card from Frankie Lee and a way to sneak out on my first date with him. After all, if you give a person a valentine card, shouldn't a date follow?

You know, there is something about the way he looks through me when he's almost next to me at my locker; we're pretty much locker neighbors, you know. And when he passes by all those girls in the hall, he tips his head in a hello way and that one little curl just dips down into his right eye. Those girls just giggle and turn their heads, but at least he looks at them. I'm not the prettiest girl in class, I'm just "peppermint without the stripes," Papa says. I'm not sure what he means, but that doesn't sound too bad to me.

Well, this morning the sun is shining with a bit of a nip in the air to take your breath away. It's certainly a cat kind of day – lazing around and soaking up the sunshine, but I can't wait. This morning is finally Valentine's Day and I have to drop down on my knees and say my special prayer one more time. The good Lord's heard it for forty-five days straight now - "Please Lord let Cupid touch Frankie Lee's heart and send to me his Valentine Card. Amen."

For school today, I've donned my special lacy red dress that Aunt Pearl B made for me, even though it is hanging around my ankles and all the other girls wear their dresses to their derriere, I look good for me. Besides Papa wouldn't let me out of the house in something bobbing off my rear end. And with that red ribbon that Aunt Fuzz tied around my

PART I: FRANKIE LEE'S HEART

Christmas present, those pickles sure were delicious, I just pull my hair up in the prettiest ponytail. And last weekend when Papa and I went to the Dollar Store, I got some of that 69-cent red lipstick, you know just like those movies stars wear on those daytime soap operas. Of course, Papa was <u>way</u> in the back of the store looking for some of that 10 - 40 stuff to go in our 1967 Volkswagen Beetle. I just can't wait to get to school to make my lips all ruby red. Red is powerful, besides it makes you stand out, you know, and Frankie Lee will surely notice me today.

Unfortunately, when I arrive at school I'm not the only girl dressed in red. Seems like every girl in Ms. Fabershine's homeroom come out looking like a blasted red candy apple. But then in walks Frankie Lee, he always arrives just as the bell rings. He's dressed in his "bad to the bone" black sweatshirt and those black tight jeans. He sure is cute.

Just as I got up, my heart starts racing faster then our old Volkswagen engine and my stomach is churning something awful. I could feel those grits making their way up. I start panting like Aunt Bertha when she was giving birth to Sister, but I just take one big breath, hold it, and march right up in front of Frankie Lee. Unfortunately, my big breath comes out in a gush in his face, and he looks at me like I was from, from; oh who cares. Anyway, I lay my hand-made Valentine card on Frankie Lee's desk and turn so fast I almost toppled over. I stumble to my desk in the back knowing my face is as red as my lips. I just couldn't look at Frankie Lee knowing what a fool I've made of myself. Besides, I heard all those girls sniggering at my back. Well, at least I don't have to say that silly prayer to God and Cupid anymore.

This is my longest day on earth.

Frankie Lee never even looked in my direction, let along acknowledged my Valentine. He just sits up front, not saying a word, just smiling. By the end of homeroom, he must have collected a card from every girl in class, and those silly girls were all giggling and carrying on over their cards.

I didn't get one card.

After my last class, I race home before Papa arrived so I could scrub that lipstick off my lips. If Papa sees me, I know I really would be in my room for a good long while.

I put on my red pajamas and commence frying up some chicken for supper when there's this knock at the front door: must be Papa forgot his keys again. Papa had to go back to the store for some more 10-40 oil for our car. That car laps up motor oil like a cat laps up cream. I take off my apron, but flour's still all over my arms and face. I yank the door open and to my surprise, standing at the door, looking prettier than I'd ever seen him, is Frankie Lee. My heart must have dropped clear out of my body, cause I know I have gone to meet Mama in that great ceiling upstairs, 'cause I've just seen a vision.

My mouth is wide-open but I couldn't get any words come out. I stand there a minute, but I have to pinch myself before any words start flowing. "Frankie Lee, is that you?" I swear words just fly out of my mouth before my brain has time to catch up. Now I know he must think I'm demented.

"Hi, LillyAnn." He smiles and his right dimple makes him look like one of those boys in that teen magazine that Margaret Ann's always carrying around.

I didn't even know Frankie Lee knew my name, but his voice sure sounds like Jimmy Lee playing that harp of his at the Saturday afternoon church social that Papa and I went to last

PART I: FRANKIE LEE'S HEART

weekend. Before I could find my voice again, Frankie Lee hands me this oversized envelope.

"I made this for you." His voice's so low and sexy.

Now I know I've died and passed right on up beyond heaven - I've stopped breathing. I didn't even get a chance to say thank you before Frankie Lee turns and heads down our drive way; leaving me standing with my mouth still open and hands trembling.

When I open the envelope, it's not what I expected. I didn't get my Valentine card. What I did get is worth more than any old Valentine card. On the front of this card is the most beautiful acrylic painted angel hovering above a girl that I think looks like me; red dress, red curly hair pulled back encircled by a red ribbon, and you know I think that is me. And when I open the card, in his own beautiful handwriting, are the words: "May you be protected each day and night as my angel watches over you for me. Your friend, Frankie Lee Studebaker."

I race upstairs, fall on my knees, and thank the good Lord for answering more than my prayers. I hide my treasure under my mattress just as Papa slammed the front door. I swear, if I close my eyes, I can still smell Frankie Lee's cologne. It has a sort of burned fragrance. Oh no the chicken, "Lord my chicken's burning."

PART II: FADE TO BLACK

Peter has my head between his hands squeezing. "Why do you make me do this to you?" Squeezing harder. "If you'd only call when you're going to be late, I wouldn't have to keep teaching you these lessons." His hands lower encasing my neck. "You make me do this!"
 I am suffocating.
 I fade to black.

❧

 When I awaken, it is morning and I am alone. Peter has left me on the floor, and as usual, fully clothed. It is only 5:00 A.M., but I quickly shower, and after applying make-up to my bruises, I leave for work at Wal-Mart, my safe haven.
 At exactly 8:30 a dozen red roses arrive from Peter. I can see the envy in my co-workers' eyes. At 8:45, I am paged. I know later I will receive another warning concerning personal phone calls.
 Peter's lazy voice greets my ears. "Hey LillyAnn."
 "Hello Peter." I catch the fear in my voice. I can see Louise's ears perking up and I hold the phone closer.
 "Just called to check on you. You know I love you."
 I internalize my sigh, "Yes." I whisper.

"What time will you be home?"

I've caught Peter glancing through my purse, so I know he knows my schedule. Anyway, I figure the time in my head and build in an extra 20 minutes. "I'll be home by 6:40."

"Don't be late. You know, I love you."

I won't. I thought to myself. Peter has already hung up.

I've had the same conversation every week since I married Peter six weeks ago.

Peter had been traveling to Chattanooga on business when he stopped in the Dollar Store to buy Tylenol. "You know you're a vision. I think you've cured my headache." His smile flirted with my heart.

I could do nothing but smile back, "That'll be $3.29." I said.

He handed me a ten and told me to keep the change. I felt my heart stop. This must be real love, I thought. I decided Peter must have city smarts, like Guy on "As the Town Turn." Two days later, he stopped by again carrying a single red rose.

Papa passed on two and a half years ago. Hit a tree head-on while almost missing a deer. My heart had not healed and I was lonely.

Peter's visits became more frequent, and thoughtlessly I fell in love with him and after a five-week courtship I stood before a justice of the peace and became Mrs. Peter Flanning. Peter had been the perfect gentleman. He never once tried to get me into bed - willing to wait until we were married.

I got married dressed in red, holding an angel Frankie Lee had given me ten years earlier. Frankie Lee had joined the marines at 17 and left high school after passing his GED test. I never heard from him again.

PART II: FADE TO BLACK

Alone in Nashville, my thoughts frequent my teenage years. Peter always makes a point of being home when I get in. Lateness is his one pet peeve. We do not spend much time together; urgent business soon takes him away after we have dinner.

I thought of my lovely hand-painted angel, I lied to Peter when I told him, "It was Papa's last gift."

"LillyAnn I made this for you." I could still see Frankie Lee's face, right dimple and all. Hear his low, shy, sexy voice.

That was my best Valentine day at age 14.

That year I prayed 45 days to Cupid and the Good Lord for Frankie Lee's Valentine Card. Papa and I didn't have much and I know now that I probably was the town joke, but Papa taught me to be proud, "peppermint without stripes" he called me.

Aunt Pearl B had made me a beautiful lacy red dress. When I tried it on, it almost reached the floor. She said, "A lady never shows a gentleman any of her unmentionables before their wedding night." Then she hugged me and wiped a tear away. Papa said she lost her little girl at birth and couldn't have any more young'ens.

That year I tied up my hair in a red pickle jar ribbon. That must have come from Aunt Fuzz; she always won the county fair first place ribbon for pickles. Then at Christmas, she'd tie a red ribbon around my pickles, "Just remember, you're always the best, LillyAnn." She'd tell me.

When I got to school that year, I put on my 69 cent fiery red lipstick that I slipped in my pocket at the Dollar Store. My heart was thumping like our old '67 Volkswagen Beetle engine; I was so afraid Papa was going to catch me. The first dollar I earned at the Dollar Store, I slipped in the cash register. A sin forgiven.

"Excuse me," a man's whispered voice interrupts my thoughts.

I tense and then realize I am still at work, "Yes, sir."

"Where can I find the Tampons?" He whispers. "For my girlfriend." He looks around, eyes darting right and left.

"Three aisles down, last shelf on the right." I whisper back.

He scurries off, still glancing for familiar faces. I glance at my watch, "Oh no, 6:30. I'll have to hurry." I run to the back to clock out, ignoring a customer, but feeling his un-approving stare.

"I'll have to hurry, I'll have to hurry," I softly repeat. Traffic on Murfreesbrough Road is moving slowly. Leaving work 21 minutes late has eradicated my built in time cushion.

I park at 6:56. My body tenses, my legs are dead weight. I walk up the six stairs to enter our condo.

Peter sits.

Tears scream down my face.

Peter rises.

I force myself to the past. *My heart was racing faster than our old Volkswagen engine and my stomach's churning something awful. I started panting like Aunt Bertha when she was giving birth to Sister, but I just took one big breath, held it, and marched right up in front. I turned so fast I toppled over. I could hear the other girls sniggering, and I couldn't look....*

This is my longest day on earth.

"Why do you make me do this to you?" His voice demands.

I see Peter's dark blank eyes. His grip tightens around my neck.

Fade to Black.

PART III: PRAY UNTIL SOMETHING HAPPENS

Peter answers the phone call as I lie in pain and silent tears. He listens with an occasional "un-huh," "sorry," "we'll be right there," "you need family now," and finally "we'll be there at 2:00."

"Get up, LillyAnn." He quietly summons, "We've business to take care of."

I obey without question listening to the unusual but familiar tone in his voice. I watch him enter my closet and carefully select my good Sunday-go-to-church-meeting dress, which I have had few occasions to wear, except in death. I shower, put on the solemn black dress, brushed back my short nasty blond hair, and wait.

The mirror reflects an image of Peter's mother, thanks to him presenting his hairdresser Wilma with the honor of transforming me into that image of the worn photo that presides in his wallet and on our mantel.

Why wasn't I surprised to read *"When you love someone with every sunrise there's pain"* on the back of that photo?

After all, Peter inflicts pain and then love.

On July 4, I watch the exchange between Wilma and Peter. His smile seems extra flirtatious, just like when I first met him. And she, being a woman, smiles back. As Peter held the picture up for Wilma to study, the scribbling on the back darts out at me.

I do not like the chemicals; they burn my nostrils and make my eyes tear. And Wilma keeps repeating, "I'm going to make you pretty for your husband." I endure the smell, noisy hair dryers, women's nosy chatter, and the insult of her implying I am ugly. I suffer to live in peace.

After the transformation, I bare a somber resemblance to Mrs. Flanning. She died two years to the date we were married.

To finish my costume for the events of the day, I apply sufficient make-up and the coral pink lipstick that Peter's niece supplies from his monthly Avone order.

Peter attires himself in a black suit, white starched shirt, and a black tie lay across the chair as his final article of clothing to adorn. He quickly spit shines his Sunday black shoes and in silence carefully pulls on his shear blue socks over the corns on his left big toe, while quietly cussing himself for having worn his good pair of black socks last night.

I adorn one-inch black pumps, sheer black stockings, and no jewelry. I sit on the end of the bed, awaiting further orders. I dare not add color to the occasion.

"LillyAnn," Peter's eyes meet mine in the mirror's reflection, as he puts the finishing touches on tying his tie. "I don't know how to tell you this." His lazy voice seems lazier.

I still met his eyes' reflection.

"That was your cousin, Betty Mai."

PART III: PRAY UNTIL SOMETHING HAPPENS

Betty Mai, she's ten years older and Aunt Fuzz's only child. I haven't heard from her since I got a graduation card containing five dollars.

"LillyAnn, did you hear me!"

When I look up, Peter's breath warms my face. "Um, um,.." I couldn't think of what to say. I try to take natural breaths.

"LillyAnn, I know you were close to your Aunt." Peter's voice has calmed.

"What?" I plea.

He lightly grabs my shoulders, "LillyAnn, I said your Aunt Fuzz died the other night. Her heart stopped. That was Betty Mai. I told her we'd be there at 2:00."

Death intrudes in my brain. "Aunt Fuzz?" A tear slithers down my cheek.

Peter sits down next to me and gathers me in his arms and kisses the top of my head. I try to relax into his arm.

"Everything's going to be alright, I always make it alright." He's cooing me like I am a child.

I could feel his hug tightening around me and I stiffen. The ones I love seem to desert me. I give in and go limp.

The ride to Rockvale is calm. So tranquillizing I could dream. I'm not sure why we're dressed in black or of what use we're supposed to be. Death is dead. I didn't want to sit up with the body and funerals make me remember. I feel someone's light touch upon my hand, *"Papa?"*

I shake my dreams away and find Peter lightly messaging my hand with his fingertips. Maybe death will bring back the Peter I dated.

Poor Betty Mai, now she's alone. Aunt Ida Mai died before Papa and Aunt Pearlie B. They say Aunt Pearlie B was handling snakes and must have not been pure of heart, but I say that copperhead must not have been too pure considering it died also. And someone said Sister wasn't born right in the brain and she poisoned her own mother for insurance money that didn't exist. Poor Aunt Bertha, she had such a time giving birth, who would have thought the life she gave would take hers.

I watch Peter. He parks. He smiles and my lips move upward.

His watch dings twice at the 2:00 hour. He descends from the driver's side of the car and walks around to open my door, smile still on his stiffen face, takes my hand gently and helps me up.

I want the moment to continue, but it's not long before Betty Mai emerges from Aunt Fuzz's house and deposits herself into Peter's stiff waiting arms. She whimpers. Betty Mai's chubby cheeks are quickly damp. "Oh Peter."

She reaches for his hands, "Thank you for coming."

I have to remind myself not to suck the lipstick off my bottom lip and keep my eyes focused. I am quickly enveloped in soft flesh. I stiffen, but force myself to relax. She pats me on the back a couple of times and then releases me.

"She'll be here soon." Betty Mai assures us.

She, Soon? I question in my mind.

"We'll be sitting up until Noon on Sunday." Betty Mai nods to Peter.

Twenty-Two hours. I thought. *At least I won't be staying.*

"Thank you, LillyAnn." Betty Mai's eyes smile at me.

I smile. Once again dreaming has caused me to miss an important fact. I watch Peter remove my small, worn, red yard

PART III: PRAY UNTIL SOMETHING HAPPENS

sale suitcase from the truck. He must have packed and put my bag in the truck while I was in the shower.

"I'll stay until your aunt comes and then I have to get back to work. LillyAnn will keep you company." Peter informs Betty Mai, flashing his winning smile.

My breath becomes quick and I close my eyes to survive. Peter and Betty Mai plan my next movements. I should be happy to be back, but somehow I lose my sense of freedom being here. Peter and I have been together for the past eight months. My innocence left behind. Whose rules shall I follow now: Peter's, Betty Mai's, or the ritual in respect of the dead?

Peter kisses the top of my forehead, "You behave now."

I knew Peter did not expect an answer; I would obey.

He hugs Betty Mai and her kiss catches the corner of Peter's lips. She smoothes her red lipstick off with her fingertip. "Thank you again Peter." A second hug and more tears. She releases her embrace. "Do you think you could come early tomorrow?" Her eyes' flirt.

He smiles and rubs her shoulders, "I'll be here," he pauses, "early."

I wonder what time is early.

Just then the black hearse pulls up from Sanders Funeral Home. Peter seems in prayer. I have never seen this expression on his face. Betty Mai starts wailing and grabs for Peter.

Dave Sanders and his son Lou unload a golden coffin. The sun hits the casket and brightness blinds me.

Mr. Sanders gives Betty Mai a conforming rub on the back, "I'm sorry for the loss of your loved one. Candice was a good woman. She shall be missed dearly. We'll set up in the parlor, if that's okay with you."

Betty Mai manages to nod her head.

Lou Sanders' blank face looks at me, "Sorry to see you under these circumstances, LillyAnn." He squeezes my hand.

Peter's eyes slant toward our hands.

"Thank you." I glance downward.

Betty Mai takes Peter's hand and follows the remains into the parlor. I follow. I catch my breath as the golden metal coffin seems the missing piece of furniture. Golden lace curtains surrounded by ruby shades adorn the center windows. The golden chandelier with jewel trim dangles above the new centerpiece. The room makes the casket look like a satin antique.

"Up?" Mr. Sanders raise the top without waiting for an answer.

"I suppose. They'll probably start coming around 4:00." Betty Mai now seems in control.

Aunt Fuzz looks like an angel covered in plastic. Her lips were in her usual upward position. I smile back. "I know Aunt Fuzz."

I feel eight eyes stare at me, but no comments are made.

"We'll be back to take care of her on Sunday." Mr. Sanders responds. "We'll be taking our leave now. Betty Mai. LillyAnn." He nods in respect to Peter.

"Well," Peter does not look at me or Aunt Fuzz, "LillyAnn, I'll see you tomorrow."

I can't take my eyes off of Aunt Fuzz. I hear her, feel her presence.

"Betty Mai, I'll see you early tomorrow."

"Thank you Peter." Betty Mai turns and starts towards Peter, but he has eased backward and made his exit.

I look out the window near Aunt Fuzz's coffin and watch as our green Chevy truck kicks up dust and disappear.

Twenty-one hours.

PART III: PRAY UNTIL SOMETHING HAPPENS

"Well, LillyAnn, let's get you settled. You can have mama's room if you like. I'm more comfortable in my old room. She hasn't changed things around in over ten years. I guess she knew I'd have to come back for her homecoming. You've got a fine husband there. You know I would have come to see you get hitched if you'd asked. But then I guess you wanted him all to yourself." Betty Mai's words ramble on.

"Any room is fine. What can I do?" I inquire.

"I guess, you could unpack, rest. I know you're probably tired." Her voice was too sweet. "When they start coming I'll get you. They always bring food, you know. Mama kept the house spotless, so there's nothing to do. Nothing at all. That husband of yours sure is nice. I wish mine had been half that nice. Maybe we'd still be together."

"Yeah." I agree, *I wish I could give him to you,* I thought.

"Being near dead people makes me nervous. I would have just stuck her in a grave if she hadn't left some paper with Mr. Sanders talking about how she wanted to be buried and orders for that dang gold coffin. That's what other folks do, you know. People don't sit up anymore. Don't have time."

Not knowing what else to do, I just smile. "I'll take my suitcase upstairs."

"You take mama's room now, my stuff's in the other one." Her voice trails after me.

Aunt Fuzz's doorknob is warm to my touch. Pickle ribbons adorn the room. Aunt Fuzz must have won every county fair contest since she was a teenager. Pickle ribbons for my hair, I thought. She even had two jars of last year's winning pickles, labeled for Christmas "Betty Mai, LillyAnn." The hand-made quilt on her bed depicts scenes from our childhood. It was probably made over a ten-year span. A Bible lay open at the head of her oak bookcase bed and she still had every card I'd made for her held together with rubber bands.

Under the cards, an oversized yellowing envelope peeks out with my name and address printed in the middle. Near the bottom she has printed, "LillyAnn, I saved these for you. Your Papa said you were too young."

My hands tremble. I close the door and sit nervously on the edge of her bed.

"Oh, Aunt Fuzz." I whisper to no one. I break the seal and pour out five letters addressed to me from Frankie Lee, U.S. Marine Corp.

I did not hear the phone ring or Betty Mai's knock, just her shout, "LillyAnn LillyAnn are you awake? Telephone."

"Yeah."

I reach for the phone.

"Just wanted to check on you before I go out." Peter's voice greets me.

"Everything's fine."

"Good. I'm meeting a client, so I won't be home until late. I'll be there tomorrow around Noon. Would you tell Betty Mai for me? I can't make it early, business, you know, comes first."

"I'm sure she'll understand."

"I love you. Now, behave yourself tonight."

"I will." I hold the phone until I heard a second click and footsteps leaving my door. I open the first letter, dated six weeks after Frankie Lee joined the Marines.

"LillyAnn?" Betty Mai's distant voice interrupts, "LillyAnn, it's almost 4:00. Don't you think you should come downstairs? I'll need you to get the door."

I glance at the first letter:

PART III: PRAY UNTIL SOMETHING HAPPENS

Dearest LillyAnn, Well, I did it. I made it through basic. Now, I'm a man and I can face anything. Well, that's what Sergeant MacReady says. I shouldn't have run away. I know that now. But when I was there I didn't know how to say what needed to be said. And after my grandmother passed on, I didn't have any place to go. I didn't want to be a burden on my parents. I never liked all that attention from those girls, but I didn't what to hurt anybody's feelings either. I tried for three years to get up some courage. And I can't seem to get the nerve up in this letter either. I know I haven't said anything. I'll write you again tomorrow. It's lights out now."

"LillyAnn? LillyAnn, I know you're not sleeping."
Knocks pound my door.
"LillyAnn?"
"I'll be right out Betty Mai."
"Okay. Someone's knocking. You've got to get the door. I can't let people think I have no one. Come on." Her voice shrilled like a baby bird.

I seal the letters back in their original container and put them under the satin throw pillow. I should look at my makeup, but no one will be here to see me.

Betty Mai sits in the far corner as the sunlight illuminates her loose, but chiseled features. She will mourn in show for her friends. After all, death is for the living. She doesn't look at me; her focus is on the door. I hear her softly whisper, "Go on." I'm not sure if she's speaking to Aunt Fuzz or me.

I smooth my dress, from habit, and open the door without checking to see the visitor.

"Oh, Betty Mai!" Ms. Hadley's arms are outstretched and Betty Mai enters. Ms. Hadley is Aunt Fuzz's pickle competition.

Ms. Hadley always took second place and her offering for the ritual tonight is a jar of pickles.

I close the door.

Two hours later the doorbell sounds. Betty Mai grits her teeth at me and rolls her eyes. I smile and rise from the polite unacquainted chatter of Ms. Hadley and Betty Mai.

"I'm so sorry for your loss. I'm Petunia." Her bleached teeth dazzle me as she hands me fried chicken and her shedding red fox throw.

"Thank you. I'm Betty Mai's cousin, LillyAnn." I take the dead creature from her and meet her smile.

"Petunia!" Betty Mai embraces the thin woman. "Oh, thank you for coming."

"You know I'm always here for you."

Their hug finally ends and they join Ms. Hadley in the far corner. No one has paid respects to Aunt Fuzz.

I retreat to the kitchen to prepare a tray of fried chicken and pickles. A knock at the back door startles me. Aunt Fuzz required children to enter in the back, but who could this be?

I can tell from the slit in the window of the back door that the sun is setting and I cannot make out the outline inquiring entrance at the back. I slowly ajar the door.

"LillyAnn?"

"Frankie Lee, is that you?" I swear words just fly out of my mouth before my brain has time to catch them.

"Hi." He smiles and his right dimple makes him look like one of the boys in those teen magazines that Margaret Ann carried in high school. "I've come to pay my respects to Aunt Fuzz."

His voice still sounds like Jimmy Lee's harp, low and sexy. Before I could find my voice again, Frankie Lee hands me this oversized envelope. "It's for Betty Mai."

PART III: PRAY UNTIL SOMETHING HAPPENS

"I'll make sure she gets it."

"You think I might come in?"

"Oh, I'm sorry, Frankie Lee. Please excuse me. I'm just, I'm sorry." I open the door and allow Frankie Lee to enter. "She's in the parlor."

"Thank you."

His uniform fits him. I'm not sure what his rank is, but he has bars and medals that are worn proudly. Halfway through the kitchen he turns and faces me. He must have felt me staring at him.

"LillyAnn?"

"Yes."

"I hope it's okay, I mean I know you're married, but I was hoping I'd see you tonight."

I feel 14 again and all I can do is smile.

"I made this for you."

My hands shake as I take the homemade envelope with little angels on the outside. Opening it, I find a card with a beautiful oil painted angel hovering above a girl with red curly hair pulled back encircled by a red ribbon with the handwritten inscription: "May you be protected each day and night as angels watch over you. I'm sorry for your loss. Frankie Lee Studebaker."

"It's beautiful. Thank you." I pause to gather my thoughts and his eyes never leave mine, "Frankie Lee, I - I mean, I didn't get, thank you." I divert my eyes thinking of Peter's rage.

His smile saddens as he turns and continues to the parlor.

The doorbell sounds, but I remain in the kitchen.

Eighteen hours.

I am startled back to reality by the slam of a tray by Betty Mai. More chicken.

"LillyAnn, what are you doing in here? You're supposed to be getting the door." She lashes out a little too loudly.

"I'm sorry." I say, then "I didn't know I was your maid." slips out of my mouth before I thought about it; then a sniff, a tear. I wipe my eyes too hard. My body stiffens for the blows.

"LillyAnn, there's just no," She stops and looks at me harshly. Her eyes squint, she steps closer. "What are those, bruises?" Her hand comes up to touch my face, but I turn my head.

I hear the squeak of the door, but I can't stop the tears. Eight months of pent up pain retch my body.

When I calm I find myself enfolded in warm arms. We are rocking and the coos slowly penetrate my soul calming me. I wipe fluid on starched material.

I focus my eyes and see Betty Mai stilled in the corner, head slightly bowed. The body I am holding is tight, strong, and muscular. I unwrap and pull back. Frankie Lee's expressionless face looks down on me.

I suck the lipstick off my lower lip.

"LillyAnn," Frankie Lee's tender voice starts as he takes out his handkerchief to wipe more tears.

Betty Mai steps up, wedging herself between us. "Frankie Lee, why don't you go to the parlor? I should take care of this." Her voice puts her in charge.

He hesitates but obeys.

"LillyAnn,.. what.. caused.. all this,.. your.. bruises?" She speaks each word distinctly and slowly.

I stare downward, grasping for my best lie.

She steps closer. "You've got yourself a real shiner."

I look upward, eyes darting past her, choosing my words cautiously, "It was dark and I tripped over my own two feet and hit my head on the bathroom doorknob."

PART III: PRAY UNTIL SOMETHING HAPPENS

"Well, then, I'm glad you've calmed yourself. Peter," she starts, "I know Peter..."

The doorbell is a welcome interruption.

"I'll get it." I needed to escape her questions.

"No! You go upstairs and fix your face." She half-smiles, patting me on the back as the flab under her arms swing. "I'll make your excuses, after all, you are taking mama's death hard and they'll understand."

She made a quick exit. I wipe my eyes and then follow. Frankie Lee held the front door open as Mrs. Pettus and two small girls enter. Betty Mai, hovering in the corner, is holding the cordless phone close and whispering. I lower my head and continue upstairs with eyes following my demure steps.

I weep and Aunt Fuzz's white satin pillow becomes my oasis smeared with lipstick, makeup, and mascara absorbed by the essence of Aunt Fuzz. "If you want something bad enough and if you haven't asked for anything in a long time, then you're deserving. Good Lord, it's been so long."

A quiet voice enlightens me, *"Be Quiet and know that I am God."* Darkness finally engulfs me and an uninterrupted sleep enters.

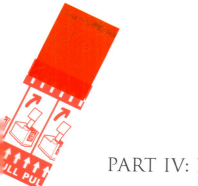

PART IV: LILYANN'S HEART

Sunshine between partially open green curtains awakens me seconds before a soft knock.

"LillyAnn? Do you want some breakfast? We've got plenty of food from last night."

"Maybe later."

"It's 8:00, you'll better start getting ready. I, I, I've talked to Peter."

Silent is my answer.

"LillyAnn?" She knocked again. "Why don't you unlock the door so we can talk? Peter's real worried about you."

"What did he say?"

"He said you have these crying spells a lot and you're not very graceful. Come on, LillyAnn, open the door."

"I'll be out in a minute." I did not want Betty Mai to intrude into the world Aunt Fuzz has left for me. I touch the envelope beneath the satin pillow.

I hear her footsteps on the stairs.

Four hours.

Peter, who gave her the right to call him? I run fingers through my blond hair and massage my neck. I retrieve Frankie Lee's letters. Instead of opening them, I hide them again. I reach for my cotton robe and head for the shower to begin my final act. The hot water pains and calms me. In the corner I see Aunt

Fuzz's Clairol Number 5 Flaming Red dye, but Aunt Fuzz always had black hair. I accept her invitation.

I look at the dark blue suit Peter has packed with little else to go with it. A Dollar General Store tag hanging out of the top drawer of Aunt Fuzz's drawer catches my eye. As I open it and borrow a pair of Aunt Fuzz's silk cream colored bra and panties still with the tags on them. They feel good.

In her closet, I spot a silk cream-colored party dress and without thinking, adore it. I unravel the towel and stare at the red head.

You look good. I'm not sure if it's Aunt Fuzz or my conscious speaking, but I do look different. Peppermint with the stripes.

My hand is guided to Maybeline Fresh Rudy Red Lipstick, a steady hand outlines and fills in my lips. Diamond studs find their way to my ears as well as its matching choker and bracelet. I step into cream-colored two-inch heels and comb my semi-wet hair. As I brush, the curls try to find their way back. I take my letters and place them on the bed by postmark dates.

Two soft knocks at my door.

"I'm almost ready Betty Mai."

There is silence, but no footsteps.

"It's, it's Frankie Lee."

I stand and become slightly dizzy. What would Peter think? I can't let him in. But my hand has already released the lock and swung open the door.

His smile catches my heart. "What are you doing here?" I stutter.

"You look beautiful."

I just smile.

"I came to see if you're okay. If you need someone to talk to."

PART IV: LILYANN'S HEART

"I'm okay."

"May I come in, Betty Mai's in the kitchen, but she probably won't be too happy when she finds out I'm not in the parlor."

"She'll tell Peter." I whisper to myself as I open the door wider and invite Frankie Lee in and in another quick motion lock it.

Frankie Lee sits beside his letters, but only glanced at them. "I like your red hair."

My hand smoothes my hair, "Thank you." I step towards the bed and found myself tripping over my feet. Frankie Lee's strong arms gathers me.

"Are you all right?"

He does not release me. But instead brings me into a standing position close to his chest.

"Yes."

Before I know what happening, he kisses me, soft and gentle. The image of Peter rushes through my head and I pull back.

"What was I thinking, I'm sorry."

"No, but I'm married." I shake my head.

Then another knock sounds at the door.

"I'll be right down Betty Mai."

"Peter's here." Betty Mai's voice intrudes my world.

"LillyAnn, let me in." Peter's voice is loud and demanding.

I couldn't help it, my body starts shaking and I blink away the tears. "He'll do bad things to me. He can't find you here."

"He's a man. No man, LillyAnn, should do harm."

"You have to hide Frankie Lee." I whisper.

Peter bangs. "That boy in there with you?"

"I had to tell him LillyAnn." Betty Mai's voice shirked in the background, "Peter will help you."

"Frankie Lee, you have to hide. He'd hurt you."

"No, I'm staying. Just open the door," more of a plea then demand.

My sweaty hand grips the door and again releases the lock. Peter swung the door open before I could fully release it. Peter's eyes budge and my heart starts racing faster than my father's old Volkswagen engine and my stomach cramps. I feel him lunge for me with hands raised.

"How dare you!" Peter yells.

But my neck is un-assaulted and I still stand. I open my eyes to find Frankie Lee standing between Peter and me. Frankie Lee's just standing. His eyes are narrow, piercing to kill.

Betty Mai is still at the door with her mouth open.

The room is too quiet.

Peter's fists are clenching and unclenching. His right hand makes a fist ready to punch, but then unfold leaving nail marks in his hand. "You want her boy?" He spats.

Frankie Lee says nothing. But that look.

"Look at her." Peter points his figure, "She's ruined herself. No self-respecting wife of mine would have red hair and a party outfit. You're at a funeral for god sake LillyAnn. I'll see about you at home." His voice trails off as he turns and quickly descends the stairs.

Betty Mai follows Peter. "I told you, what did I tell you? She doesn't deserve a fine man like you Peter. Let me fix you some chicken."

The front door slams and I watch our old truck kick dust down the road.

The uncontrollable silent tears flow. "What am I going to do, I can't go home now. Peter'll kill me."

PART IV: LILYANN'S HEART

"Then don't go back."

"Frankie Lee, you don't understand. It doesn't matter where I go, unless you're planning on standing guard, Peter will find me."

"Then I'll stay."

"But you're a marine!"

"Only for another week. My tour of duty is up. My father wants me to help him in his furniture business. I'll get him to look in on you until I return. I promise you I'll be here for you."

"But I'm married!"

"Any man that lays a hand on - beats a woman is not married. You're not his property and he can't take his problems out on you."

I could only wipe tears and stare.

Frankie Lee glances at his letters on Aunt Fuzz's bed. "Did you have a chance to read my letters?"

"You knew I didn't get them?"

"Aunt Fuzz wrote to me. We became really good pen pals. She told me she'd save them for you even after I found out you were married and I asked her to destroy them." A silent moment passed, "I always loved you and if my love now only means that I'm supposed to protect you, then that's my mission."

In his arms I weep.

"LillyAnn," Betty Mai's soft voice interrupts. "Dave and Lou Sanders are here. I just left the door open so people could enter. Do you think you could say something nice about Mama?"

A soft breeze touches my face.

"You know she left you this house. She knew I could never live in this small town, in this old house. Gosh, this house must be over a 100 years old. You've got spirits walking the floor at night. Mean ghosts too. Besides, I think Peter's pretty upset right now, so it might be best if you didn't go back, at least right now. I'll go to Nashville and get some of your things. If that's okay? He did confide in me that he thought you had probably been screwing around. And, I hate to say this, he's thinking about divorcing you. I think that might be best, you know with all that's happened. A divorce, I mean. I know of a good attorney. You don't have any kids, so it will be quick. I can go for your things, if you like."

I shake, but a warm breeze touches my cheek again. Frankie Lee hasn't released my hand. "Thank you Betty Mai and I'll be happy to say a few words for Aunt Fuzz."

As we descend the downstairs sweet voices greet us - Aunt Fuzz's final guests.

QUICK
AS
A BREATH

PART I - DEATH PLAYS INSIDE MY HEAD

As quick as a breath
Death stood at my door
Demanding royal treatment
Seeking the ultimate
Getting inside my head.

My father died in church last Sunday on April 1, 2001, of a massive heart attack. He was 40. I guess there was nothing going on in Murfreesbrough, because Doug M. Simms made front page news in the *News Element*. The headline that Monday read, "He Met His Maker." *The News Element* even had an old photograph of him in his Air Force uniform taken 20 years earlier outside some church in Kentucky. His finger was raised upward and his smile wide, as the snow lightly fell. Mama said he took the Polaroid right after he found out he had a second baby girl.

I tried to cry. But I hadn't seen him since I was eighteen and the tears just wouldn't come. I couldn't make fake ones, not even for my mother. She cried, she hollered, and she even attempted a fainting spell before two strong hands holstered her up.

My parents had only moved back together as their first daughter's death had torn them apart. Death had proved me right in 1999; they only had room in their hearts for Jasmine.

Mother had been intent on having Doug's viewing and funeral on Saturday at Second Avenue Baptist Church. She knew that the Simms had already booked the most prestigious church in Murfreesbrough for that date. A Simms' wedding had been planned six months ago at Second Avenue and Doug's sister's child, Antoinette, was to be the bride. "The dead could wait one more day, after all, Antoinette's 37 and time waits on no living person. Doug would have understood," Elder Louis, Doug's brother, pled.

But mother would not bend to their wishes and the funeral was set for Saturday at the exact hour of Antoinette's wedding at the smaller surroundings of Cartwright Funeral Home for the going home celebration.

In her mind, Mother was the victim, as Doug's siblings: Elder Louis, Loretta Ann and Kellie Mae, stayed away to attend the wedding festivities. They opted for a private ceremony honoring Doug the night before.

Mother told every one of their unkind words and their unwillingness to accept what would have been Doug's wishes and, of course, her eyes grew weary as she gathered her friends' words of compassion.

11:00 A.M. Saturday, Cartwright Funeral Home.

I stood out in my red micro-mini dress in the sea of blackness. They whispered behind my back, inside my head, *"How dare she wear that to her own father's funeral!"* Their voices intentionally carried. I learned to face my enemies early in life and as the family marched solemnly in to view the last remains of Douglas Malcolm Simms, I confronted the onlookers' eyes until they looked away and pretended a tear, bowing their heads.

PART I - DEATH PLAYS INSIDE MY HEAD

IT started deep down within her. I remembered hearing that low musical wail when I was fifteen after Grandma Simms's pacemaker refused to restart her body. My mama could "shout" with the best on a Sunday morning. She even cleared out the church when I was ten.

IT grew.

And by the time she reached the coffin the whole church was filled with her high pitched shrill. The ushers, with their white purity uniforms, nurses' shoes, white stockings, and long white gloves, pulled her up and slightly lifted her to the front row pew where she was surrounded by her friends. I took my place on the second row as the funeral attendant hid my father's face. I smiled at the thought of his peaceful face.

Death was not painful, for the dead felt no pain. And I did not fear the dead. I admired their ability to be silent.

A loved one touched,
A heart demolished,
Tears for the living,
Death's getting inside my head.

The minister of Second Avenue Baptist Church, Pastor Smithe, chose to celebrate Doug's homecoming, instead of the Simms's wedding, Pastor Smithe chose to feed lies to the spectators, white lies, for my mother's sake and my inheritance. He wouldn't embarrass her in front of her friends, family, and neighbors, and his congregation needed my organ. Mama had kept ours in mint condition; not even allowing us to take lessons or sit on the beautiful stool of the instrument. I always thought she would do the decent thing and pass my Estey

Virtuoso Organ down to me as my Granny and Great Granny did for her.

The sermon was short. "He was a good man and good father and husband." The type of sermon you hear when the minister was not familiar with the deceased. I gazed at the Pastor, but he did not return my eye contact. He was in what I called a minister's zone. When I was ten he baptized me claiming to save me from the throat of hell. Not saying I'm not back there now. After Reverend Smithe's voice started that hissing-sinus sound, I quit listening. The babble made the little hairs on the back of my neck stand up.

I focused my attention on the Obituary. My whole name was listed: Caroline Hortensia (Hor), Nashville. Of course, I legally changed my name on my 18th birthday. I am Swann. But here, I was Annie's daughter. She showed me off like a trophy, then discarded me as others centered on her focus.

At the gesture of Reverend Smithe, the congregation stood. The flower girls, honorary pall bearers, and pall bearers formed the funeral procession followed closely by the family. Mama, with silent tears, followed Doug; held up by too friendly hands perched upon her shoulder. I put on my red sunglasses and follow. The sun greeted my too red lips, making my dress look fiery.

I am Swann. Caroline died upon the death of my sister; the murder of my sister, and the final rejection of my mother and pretend father. I left as others followed the coffin. I am sure Doug M. Simms agreed with my decision to not linger. I am not a good Baptist.

Death stands at my door
Getting royal treatment inside my head,

PART I - DEATH PLAYS INSIDE MY HEAD

If life exists for the living,
Who then is death for, if not the living?

I had kissed Jasmine to death
then whispered "Good-night."
I do not fear the dead.

Death to Death.

PART II - FIRST BORN

1999

Jasmine is my older sister by exactly ten months and twenty-nine days, and from the day I could rationalize, I wanted her dead.

When Jasmine was sixteen, I overheard Jules, one of Daddy's young associates, reveal to Jasmine that she was an arrangement that could unhinge men's minds. Unfortunately Daddy, appearing from behind the door, enlightened Jules that if he desired to make partner in his law firm that he had better keep his opinions and eyes to himself. Of course, Jules mysteriously tendered his resignation the following week.

From that day on Jasmine seemed to know the effect she had on men and how to use her looks to get what she wanted.

I am Caroline Hortensia Simms, oh you would have thought my parents could come up with a better name for their second born child. And my nicknames make me cringe every time my family affectionately called me Hor or Horten. I did not emulate any of my sister's attributes: I stood too tall, looked like I was anorexic, and at first glance my face lacked feminine appeal. But at least I developed a streak of independence.

Jasmine spent her younger years watching cartoons, reruns of <u>Beverly Hillbillies</u>, and with the help of mother, developing her feminine appeal. Her favorite saying was "Daddy I need," and what Jasmine wanted, Jasmine got. Jasmine was good at twisting men around and convincing them they wanted to give her everything. When she was little she projected this angelic smile; but as her body matured she demanded the attention of a woman and the way my sister learned to control men's minds.

On the other hand, I worked since I was sixteen at Middle Tennessee Medical Hospital in the dialysis center as a reuse technician and still managed to maintain a 4.0 G.P.A. But nothing I did seemed to please Daddy. I earned academic scholarships and saved enough money to carry the entire financial burden of college. Were they thankful? They were too busy trying to please their favorite child. They gave her everything, including doubling her allowance when I started working.

When I was eight, I watched my first <u>Perry Mason</u> rerun and I was absorbed. Daddy thought it was funny that an eight-year-old would rather watch <u>Perry Mason</u> instead of cartoons. But my interest evolved around the murderer and how he calculated, plotted, and carried out the crime without one twinge of guilt. And from my first show, I knew I could murder my sister without guilt, and since there was no real Perry Mason and most cold blooded killers were thought to be men, I would survive. My journal became my murder diary. While Jasmine watched cartoon after cartoon, I wrote down murder plots, studied real crimes, and explored where the evidence lead to conviction. One day, Jasmine would be my victim.

After high school graduation, my sister took a year off from school convincing Daddy she needed to "find" herself. She spent the whole year partying, dating every guy in Murfreesbrough,

PART II - FIRST BORN

Tennessee, and lazing around. All the time she pretended to be Daddy's perfect little innocent girl. For graduation, Jasmine got a brand new fire red Ford Mustang Convertible. A year later, I got Daddy's eight-year-old, half-rusty Volkswagen Rabbit. Then when she saw how happy Daddy was that I was going to UT Knox, Jasmine applied and can you believe they accepted her.

Why wouldn't she just leave me alone?

She even talked her latest love Joseph, who was also a graduating senior, into following her to UT. In her quest to be a "perfect" sister, or was it more of a bitch, she shared with me the one secret of getting your next man was to make others think you were unattainable. I felt sorry for Joseph. Unfortunately for him, he was her favorite type: muscular, tall, tan, dark hair, C student, and the most important ingredient, wealthy parents who saw beauty as god's gift to their genes.

I knew it would only be a matter of days before Jasmine dumped poor Joseph.

For me, I had one true love, Michael. He graduated a year before me and, of course, went to UT. I met Michael when I was a freshman at Riverside High School. I knew we were meant to be and our passion for science brought us together on various school projects. Our relationship, though never physical, bloomed during our three school years together; and on the written page as letter after letter we declared our love during Michael's time away. While Michael did his summer internship in Texas, his letters became less frequent, but finally we were going to be together.

In my lifetime, I had only three boyfriends, counting Michael. The others did not last long before Jasmine played her game to win them over, only to drop them days later.

Fortunately for me, Michael was not Jasmine's type. Michael was too intelligent and on the skinny side, plus money and beauty were not his main motivation in life.

Arriving at the University, Jasmine stayed under foot, insisting on doing everything together, "just like real sisters were supposed to do," she smiled. But standing next to me, her beauty exuded even more outrageously.

For my sanity, I put every effort into being the good sister my father always expected. I made arrangements to meet Michael and Joseph at "A-Jay's Restaurant and Lounge".

Unfortunately, my sister decided the time had already come to look for Joseph's replacement. I delicately tried to tell her how ridiculous she looked in that short red dressed. "Jasmine, you know your breasts are hanging out of that dress. I mean your dress is too tight. I mean, you know, we're supposed to be meeting the guys at A-Jay's, not going to a fraternity party."

I was dressed in a baggy Titan's T-shirt and black jeans held up by elastic in the waist trying to hide the shape that was missing.

Jasmine projected her usual devious smile, "I've just decided he's history - there are too many classy rich guys around. So, you know, I have to advertise. How can you buy the merchandise if you can't see the product? One look at me and men can tell I don't come cheap." Jasmine accentuated her outfit with black nylons, garter belt, and 4 inch red stilettos.

Her smile was making me sick so I snarled at her, "Jasmine, I can't believe we're sisters."

She half laughed, "Of course not, you're adopted."

This was the taunt Jasmine had used to keep me off balanced since I was seven. My face betrayed me as disbelief and horror shrieked across.

PART II - FIRST BORN

Jasmine laughed and said her usual, "Just kidding." She patted me on the head and turned to apply her ruby red lipstick to match her dress.

"Don't joke like that!" I retorted. I really did believe I was adopted.

It was early and A-Jay's was sparsely crowded, mostly with five or six girls surrounding one guy. Their giggles intruded my thoughts as we walked in.

I saw Michael for the first time in over a year. I was surprised and frightened and almost didn't recognize him. During our separation, Michael had bulked-up and was no longer my skinny little boyfriend. He now looked like the kind of man my sister instantly latched onto. How could a person develop so many muscles in one year? God, he looked good enough to devour.

I couldn't believe he looked straight past me and into Jasmine's flirting eyes. Didn't she recognize him? He's mine.

Strategically, I had always managed to keep Michael away from Jasmine. They had only met once when she was just beginning to discover her alluring magnetism over men, but now next to my sister, I felted too thin, too tall, and not quite woman enough. I know she has the striking body of the goddess of love but true love will overcome anything.

I tried to greet Michael by giving him our traditional "bear" hug and "snuggle" face, but Michael's arms barely reacted.

"Caroline." Michael's trance like voice weakly greeted me.

I kissed Michael's cheek but his eyes elevated straight towards my sister's assets.

I watched my sister as Joseph greeted her.

"Hi, Jas." Joseph's big smile did not seem to penetrate Jasmine's gaze. Jasmine simply looked at Joseph, rolled her eyes at him, tossed her long weaved blond hair over her shoulder, and smiled at Michael.

I knew what was coming next.

"Hi, Michael." Jasmine said in her most sultry voice.

"Hi, Jasmine." Michael let go of me, but then again he never really acknowledged me. His smile enfolded her.

My sister's walk always started her consumption of a man. Now she was using it on my beloved. I had seen her work her seductive spell too many times. I loved Michael, how could she do this to me again? I closed my eyes and remembered all of Jasmine's conquests. I never understood why she wanted me along, until today: the contrast of beautiful and plain. Jasmine started her approach on Michael: her sensual smile, an extra long handshake, the touch of his cheek. Jasmine was always ready to play the confidant and best friend. And Jasmine was something all men wanted. Her seductive beauty completed every man's fantasy. Whereas, I was the crumbled cookie left in the cookie jar that no one wanted. I studied my sister's ways with men and knew when her natural instincts took over. She turned into catnip.

I felt the awkward moment. And unfortunately, today the only advertising Jasmine was doing was directed towards Michael.

"Please God, let him look at me, prove Michael is stronger than most." My prayer went unanswered.

"Why don't we sit down?" I murmured while still trying to engage Michael's eyes.

Michael took the booth and Jasmine moved within his space. I took the seat on the opposite side and stared. Michael seemed to be inhaling Jasmine's sensual aroma or was it catnip for men? They whispered and every once and awhile,

PART II - FIRST BORN

Michael looked my way as if he had forgotten I was there. He said nothing, just half smiled and turned back to Jasmine and continued whispering. Jasmine giggled and kept bringing her hand up to delicately massaging Michael's face with her fingertips. I felt like an intruder, but he was mine. Joseph hadn't bothered to sit down, just muttered something about getting sodas.

I considered myself intelligent, until it came to men. I always lost to my big sister. She accentuated perfection to the point that no one could compete.

Jasmine and Michael were still in intense conversation and flirtation purposefully keeping their voices low when Joseph dropped off the soft drinks. He tried kissing Jasmine on the cheek but she pulled closer to Michael and said nothing, literally stared him into leaving. He did.

I felt lost and after about an hour of just sitting and gawking at them, I walked back to Clement Hall. Michael did not bother to look up - not even when I whispered to him, "I love you," as I walked out.

To keep from totally losing my sanity, I did what I always did. I wrote in my diary a carefully plotted scene to murder my sister. I no longer needed murder mysteries to develop my plots. There were never tears for me; I was the stronger of the two.

Three hours later, at midnight, I went to bed. Jasmine still had not returned from A Jay's. I sensed Michael was now snarled in her web. How could he have instantly fallen for her? Was that attraction always there and I never wanted to see it?

I knew it was a mistake to be roommates with my sister, but Daddy and Jasmine had insisted. *"It will be fun."* Daddy seemed so happy his two girls would be roommates. *"You can take care of each other."* I didn't need or want taking care of.

Our room seemed to reap of Jasmine. She brought every stuffed animal she ever owned. She claimed it made the room feel more like home. And she had posters of Tom Cruise, that "cute" actor, covering her side of the room and mine. And hanging on our door was a life size picture of Snoops, her white and black Manx cat. I hated Snoops and if I had my choice, Snoops would be the subject of my next scientific experiment. I despised this room as much as I hated sharing it with my sister. I hid my diary deep between my mattresses.

In high school I loved science and decided on my major in genetic engineering. Jasmine claimed she was undecided, but I knew she had planned on majoring in men and marrying the richest one she could find. But somehow Michael was now in her sight. I admit I wasn't quite over the fact that he had turned to her so quick and so easy.

With my test scores, I went straight to advanced genetic chemistry. This class allowed freedom in my experiments, as long as I kept a journal. I spent my time imagining myself the famous scientist breaking the genetic code to invent the ultimate cure for cancer, cloning myself, and inventing an undetectable murder weapon, all in the name of advancing science.

After classes started, I did not see much of Jasmine or Michael.

PART II - FIRST BORN

My solace was my part-time job in the experimental lab where new drugs were tested. I put in extra hours, committing myself to inhaling knowledge to perpetrate the perfect crime.

Jasmine usually returned to the dorm after I was asleep and was never up when I left. We existed in two separate worlds.

On the weekends, I tried not to speak to my sister.

Jasmine pretended or maybe she did miss being her version of sisters. Her main conversation consisted of giving me tips on how to get a man, how to keep a man, nail polish, and clothes. As much as I loathed her, she had this way of getting under my skin. Can she really believe she never hurt me? I guess in my heart I knew she was just being Jasmine - getting what she wanted since birth.

I was dressed and ready to leave when Jasmine turned over and smiled. She timidly asked, "Caroline, what've you been up to lately?"

"Work and classes, but you wouldn't know anything about that? By the way, how's Michael?" I just had to know, part of me (my heart) still wanted him.

Jasmine snickered and said, "I wouldn't know; I dropped him a couple of weeks ago. Michael may have become gorgeous, but he still wants to be a scientist." She cringed. "I'm dating Cal, the senior quarterback." She stared deep within me and in her kinder voice, which usually came when I was supposed to forgive her, said, "Hor, I never took Michael from you. He came after me like a little puppy wagging his tail. I just smiled and devoured him. I did you a favor. Besides, Michael didn't call you after I dropped him because he no longer or never loved you. He used me as an excuse to leave you. Besides, you wouldn't want him back after he abandoned you upon just seeing me?"

My face felt like it had turned three shades of red. I couldn't think and all I could stammer was, "Why would I want him after you've used him?" Still a small part of me desired to be back with him.

"Well, little sister, I'm the ultimate, no man can resist me. You should know that." Jasmine shrugged her shoulders and clicked on the television.

I grabbed my books and left for the sanctuary of my lab to continue doing research on KAO, a new drug that I invented and was performing my final tests on. I turned on the lights and enjoyed the emptiness of my retreat. KAO was odorless, tasteless, undetectable, and mixed with water the rats gulped it up. Just as I imagined Jasmine would do. In the right dose, KAO was thought to stop a heart attack, but too much might induced one.

I put the vial of KAO securely into my small black leather pouch and slipped it into my purse. I filled an empty vial with water and inserted the red KAO-012435 label I had prepared the night before. I looked at the clear liquid and imagined how I would kill my dearly beloved, man-stealing sister. I would pretend to be nice and offer to get breakfast. After all, Jasmine was always trying to "make like a sister". This way she would think I had finally forgiven her. I would bring her favorite blueberry bagel and French vanilla coffee, into which I would mix KAO. Jasmine had to have caffeine every morning. After Jasmine had finished the coffee, I would leave the dorm for several hours, giving KAO time to work. Then I would return...

Walter, the senior lab supervisor, walked in, and I quickly dropped the imitator and watched it shatter into pieces. The label survived.

"Walter, you startled me!"

PART II - FIRST BORN

"Sorry. Just make sure you log it in your journal."

I held my smile.

"And Simms?"

I could feel my heart pacing. "Yes."

"You know the rule, you break it, you clean it up."

With that, Walter walked to the back. The rest of my plan began to formulate in my mental murder diary. I smiled.

I didn't speak to Jasmine for eight more days. It drove her crazy to think I was mad at her: the little sister who always forgave her. As usual, she kept smiling.

On Friday night while watching old reruns of <u>Perry Mason</u>, I knew it was time for my sister to die. That night I set my alarm for 9:00 A.M. Sweet dreams danced in my head as I lingered between sleep and thinking. After ten years of planning in my diary, I was ready to act. Sunday would be the perfect day for a murder.

Saturday, 8:30 A.M., I was up before my alarm sounded and I watched Jasmine softly snore.

Loudly, I sang, "Let me tell you a story about a girl named Jas," even louder and more off-key, "she tried to be a sister but she always failed."

Jasmine sat straight up.

"Good morning, Jasmine."

"Hor," Jasmine was now her usual chipper self with her fake Ms. America smile, "Good morning."

"Hey, since it's your birthday today, let me take you to a movie?" I sweetly smiled at her.

"How sweet. I thought you had forgotten. I have a date." Jasmine added quickly, "But we could do something early. What do you have in mind?"

"Are you still seeing Cal?"

"No, just shopping around." After a brief silence, she added as an afterthought, "Oh, Michael keeps calling and begging. Michael's sweet, but I don't think so." She turned up her nose.

"Yeah." I didn't want to hear about Michael. "How's about a movie at 1:00? That way I won't ruin your plans." It was hard keeping a smile on my face.

"Sure." She meekly agreed. "I never turn down anything free."

I had bought movie tickets at the Campus Cinema earlier and took Jasmine to see <u>Malice</u>; a thriller about an arrogant surgeon, which I knew my sister would hate.

"How did you like the movie?" I asked, trying to hide my laughter.

"Well, it wasn't the <u>Beverly Hillbillies Movie</u>."

"If that's still showing next weekend, maybe we can see it. By the way, breakfast is on me in the morning."

"Really?"

"Don't thank me; I'm just a "good" sister."

"Okay." Jasmine didn't utter another word. She dressed in tight black leather pants that showed off her pierced bellybutton and a low cut red top, said a quick good-bye and raced out.

8:00 A.M. Sunday, I dressed in my simple black dress, then left and purchased blueberry bagels, French onion cream cheese, and French vanilla coffee. I stopped in the downstairs bathroom to add the KAO to the container. I contemplated ways of waking my sister, but when I opened our door, I was surprised to find Jasmine watching cartoons in her robe.

I plastered a big smile on and greeted Jasmine's last day. "Good Morning! Breakfast as promised."

PART II - FIRST BORN

"French vanilla, it smells heavenly. Thanks Caroline. You are going to church?"

"As usual. Let me pour you a cup before I leave." I steadied my hand and sat the container down by Jasmine's cat coffee cup.

"That's okay, I'm going to change clothes and, you know. You should probably go before you're late." That smile again.

"It's no problem, I have plenty of time."

"Oh, you've already done enough. Besides you still have your gloves and coat on. Go on. I know you like the early service. Thanks for breakfast." Her voice hurried me out the door.

"Okay, enjoy your breakfast and drink your coffee before it gets cold." I slowly started for the door, hoping to see the dark liquid encounter her cup.

"I will." She turned her attention back to Underdog.

I did not want to make Jasmine suspicious, so I left to ask for forgiveness for the sin I was about to commit. Just as I got off the elevator, a chill rushed through me. I shut my eyes and calmed my mind. *Unshakable. Be quiet.* But guilt still consumed me. What was I thinking? I couldn't put my only sister to death. My breath heaved. I paced. Prayed - *Dear Father* - Pushed the up button. Tears stung the side of my eyes.

As I exited the elevator, I saw Michael enter our room. I wiped my tear, took off my shoes and walked softly. They were so busy kissing they did not hear the door being slightly opened.

Michael not only kissed her on the lips, but on both cheeks; just like he used to kiss me. He whispered something into her ear. I heard the laughter and knew it was about me. *Dear old Caroline, what a fool she is.*

I could see Michael looking around. He held her in his arms and looked deep into her eyes, then his words sung out, "I just couldn't wait to see you again. You know you are so beautiful." He glanced around again and I stepped back. "Caroline's gone?"

"Of course silly, I always time it perfectly. And don't worry by now she's probably down on her knees praying for who knows what? Relax, I brought some of your favorite coffee." Jasmine released her robe and was now dressed in her sheer red teddy that accentuated her long muscular legs, and didn't cover much of her other assets.

Michael's eyes devoured her. "You've already taken the chill off, but since you went to so much trouble I'll have some and then..."

Jasmine laughed lightly, tilting her head back. I could see the gold crown on her back tooth.

Come on Jasmine pour the coffee, I consciously coached.

Jasmine teasingly turned, showing off her backside. "I did get it especially for you." Her voice began to vibrate in my head.

That's my sister, always taking the credit. I sighed a little too loud and thought surely I was caught but they were entranced in the moment. Jasmine had poured the coffee and after taking a few sips, handed it to Michael. He nibbled on her neck. She took her cup and seemed to lap up the coffee. The brown liquid spilled as the cup tumbled to the floor.

My conscience told me I should help her, but instead I kept staring. Jasmine wiggled her shoulders allowing her straps to fall. Michael moved in front of my sister. I held my breath unable to make my feet or mouth move. I couldn't see her. Michael nibbled Jasmine's ear, shoulder, and breast.

Tears slipped down my cheeks.

PART II - FIRST BORN

They deserved each other, I reasoned as I wiped my pain away.

I shut the door and took the stairs. I wondered if Jasmine would understand the reason I was still wearing gloves. In my heart, I hoped with Jasmine's last breath she would realize that her little sister had terminated her. As I exited through the side door, I left for Mt. Zion to pray for the sin I had committed; to fall on my knees finally transformed.

Murder diary closed.

IN A BOTTLE

"Beer," she shook her head, held her bottle high, and giggled. "No, whisky's an acquired taste!" Slamming the half-empty Jack Daniel's bottle down, watching her glass tip off the table and shatter into pieces, the tiny redhead dragged her right thumb over a raw edge. Dark red liquid dripped from her cut. Showing all the restaurant onlookers her thumb, she loudly muttered, "Now this is for real drinkers!" She seemed hypnotized as her fingers advanced toward her heart-shaped face. Sucking as if her thumb were her pacifier, a single teardrop escaped.

The stares returned as strangers angled their heads to glare at her. Her bright green cowboy boots didn't match her purple almost-see-through sundress, or her knee-high socks. She was a mixture of her favorite colors.

Her waiter, who had turned his eyes as she first lifted her Budweiser then her oversized liquor bottle out of her purse, now had to take action. BYOB was not allowed at Fitzgerald's. With her half order of fried green tomatoes and all eyes beholding her, he approached.

"Ma'am, are you hurt?"

She took her thumb out of her mouth and the steady flow of blood continued. With swimmingly drunk dark questionable eyes, she held her thumb up for him to exam as she whispered, "Cherri."

Seeming a bit confused, he only returned her whispers, "I'm sorry, I didn't hear you." He leaned closer.

"My name is Cherri Jubilee!" Her full round lips matched the red of her socks as she shouted for the whole restaurant to hear.

Whispers, whispers, all the room whispered.

The air was perfumed with Tennessee whisky as the busboy silently swabbed the liquid gold from the now stained floor. Unlike the busboy, the audience gave their complete attention to Cherri, waiting to see if the strangely clothed girl would continue with the performance of the evening.

Cherri and her waiter appeared swept up in a world where their eyes communicated the next scene.

"Butch." He leaned his long hefty body over and took her reddened thumb. Gently, he wiped the blood onto his white shirttail. He then took her thumb between his opposing fingers and applied pressure. A single teardrop again escaped from her overly large brown eyes.

Time stood still. Whispers grew boisterous again as the crowd tired of the performance and returned to their now cold cuisine.

Cherri looked past Butch to see a taller, darker, impressive gentleman fidgeting behind Butch.

"Jason Carlo Fitzgerald." The man's deep baritone voice devoured the room and the spectators returned.

Butch's smile disappeared as his eyes sank. He turned his six-foot frame and looked upward. "Dad." Butch nodded and stepped sideways and allowed his father to enter Cherri's world.

As usual, his father said nothing more to Butch, instead he motioned Butch to leave and addressed the still smiling Cherri, "I'm Mr. Fitzgerald and you are?"

"Cherri."

"Cherri, did you hurt yourself?" Mr. Fitzgerald delicately stated, but Cherri understood the blame laid with her.

Cherri's happy face faded as she hid her thumb under her napkin. "I'm okay." She softly murmured.

"Well Cherri, we have a policy that no outside alcohol is allowed." Mr. Fitzgerald's stern face held Cherri's attention but his voice was so gentle it was almost a fatherly whisper. "I'll have your waiter bring you some coffee and we'll make sure you get home." Nothing more was said. He weakly smiled, then found Butch watching.

As Mr. Fitzgerald passed his son, he breathed, "Take care of this quietly and quickly."

Cherri held back the tears she knew would soon flood her cheeks. Her audience seemed to feel her embarrassment and no longer faced her. Their heads lower as Mr. Fitzgerald passed returning to his position.

Butch took a seat beside Cherri, sat down a cup, and poured half a cup of the blackest coffee Cherri had seen.

"I don't like coffee and my finger hurts." Cherri said between sniffles.

"Pretend." Butch then filled the remainder of her cup with chocolate, three tablespoons of sugar, and two spoonfuls of cream. "My special blend, give it a try. Please?"

Cherri smelled the liqueur and took a small sip. "Um, it tastes like a warm chocolate shake."

"It's my elixir of life." Butch's sultry voice proclaimed.

Cherri relaxed in his presence. "I thought you said your name was Butch."

"It is, to my friends." In a softer tone he added, "Are you really all right?"

"Getting there." She half-smiled.

"Mr. Fitzgerald, my Dad, ordered me to get you out of here. I get off in," Butch glanced at his Winnie the Pooh watch, "five minutes. Why don't I attend to my official duty and take you home?"

The tears were back, "I don't have a home." Cherri now more subdued, glanced around to see if anyone else heard her. Cherri felt the naked space that for the past twelve years had held her gold wedding band. "I guess I'm officially homeless." She took another sip of her warm chocolate coffee shake and stared into the dark liquid for answers.

Butch sensed his father's stare. "Okay. I have a car." He seemed to be feeling for words, "Why don't we just get out of here and go for a ride? I promise you I'm perfectly harmless, I've had all my shots, I won't bite, but if I do, you won't turn into a werewolf."

Her brown eyes smiled through her fears and she found her purple dress, green cowboy boots, red socks smile. "Um, werewolf, that might not be such a bad idea right now."

Butch rose, took her hand, and nodded at his father. The petite redhead stood as her braids swayed forward. Mr. Fitzgerald frowned as they left his restaurant.

"You don't have to support me. I've only had one beer." She laughed as Butch let go of her hand and almost tripped.

He stopped and looked at her, "What about the Jack Daniel's?"

"I don't like whisky. I wanted to see if I could... Think of it as an experiment; seeing the reaction of all those snobby people in your restaurant as I deliberately break a whisky bottle on your expensive floor."

Butch was silent as they again walked to the parking section behind the restaurant.

Cherri smiled and hummed.

"So that was just an act?" He paused and slowed his pace, "Why?"

"Not all of it. My thumb still hurts. And you..." She paused contemplating her thoughts, "Besides," her voice lowered as her head sank, "your father scared me; I thought he was going to have me arrested. I don't have any money." She nervously glanced around to make sure no one else approached them, "And my credit cards..." She stopped and glanced upward. Butch's face was expressionless.

Cherri wished her honesty would stop. She looked into his blank face and appeared to be asking his forgiveness, "I don't know why. I used to be among the snobbish that frequented the over-priced, over-class Fitzgerald's. Then about two months ago my husband walked out. He just left me."

"Sorry." Butch started moving through the employee parking lot searching for his vehicle.

"Don't be. Better now while I still have my youth and beauty than twenty years from now, when the kids we couldn't have are almost grown and he just can't take looking at me a second more." She had stopped and was staring into darkness as she envisioned what her future could have been. She wiped the tears from her face before Butch noticed.

Butch turned and gazed upon the woman he thought needed rescuing. "My car's over there." He pointed.

Cherri started walking behind Butch trying to match his stride.

Butch jerked off his tie and loosen the top button of his shirt as he unlocked his white 1986 Toyota Corolla. "I'm sure it doesn't compare to what you're used to, but it's all I've got." Butch's voice echoed in harshness.

Cherri stood back and eyed his car under the street light. She smiled, "Looks perfect to me, remember, I'm homeless."

"Get in. Where should I drop you off?" He refused to look at Cherri.

"You promised me a ride. You are good for your word?"

Butch started the car, closed his eyes, and paused to listen to his engine purr. He had rebuilt the engine himself - nothing pleased him more than grease under his nails. "I don't like being used." He intentionally avoided Cherri's stare.

"I didn't use you. Everyone else, maybe," she hesitated, "but not you."

"I don't remember seeing you at Fitzgerald's before?"

"I had processed straight blond hair and I dressed like all the other women. My make-up, hair, shoes, clothes, and attitude were like your usual patrons. Cloned. You wouldn't have noticed me. I was supposed to blend in, fit the mold. And I did. I have seen you before. I requested your table tonight."

Butch tried to suppress a smile. "I'm shocked they let you in tonight."

"I made reservations under my husband's name for two. When I got there I sort of hinted I was his mistress."

Butch silenced a laugh.

"Whatever happened to your mother? She was always polite to me."

Butch let out a loud sigh, "She finally left us."

"I'm sorry."

"Don't be. It was survival." They rode in silence for the next few minutes.

Cherri reclined her seat and closed her eyes.

Butch drove slowly, obeying all the traffic laws. He stole glances of Cherri as she slept and wondered if she actually was a lost soul. With no place left to drive, Butch parked at his apartment complex. "Cherri? Cherri?" Butch lightly touched her shoulder and with fingertips nudged her. "Cherri?"

Cherri opened her eyes and stared. Then a smile reappeared. "Butch." Sitting up, she looked around, "Where are we?"

"Well, I got tired of driving nowhere so we're at my place. You can spend the night, but when morning comes, you'll have to find somewhere else to stay. I need to get some sleep. It's late and I have classes tomorrow."

"Classes, you're in school?" An unbelievable tone chastened Cherri's voice.

"Yeah. Fitzgerald's is my Dad's. I'm a waiter working my way through school. It's called survival"

"How young are you?"

"Old enough."

"That means you're under 21?"

"I'm twenty-one. I've basically been on my own since I was seventeen." Butch's voice trailed off as he stared into the darkness. He turned to genuinely look at Cherri. "So, how old are you?"

"Well, I'm 30." Cherri's voice was hollow as she continued. "I turned 30 the day my husband walked out on me for an eighteen-year-old. I'm old."

Butch stole a sideway glance of Cherri. He saw no crow's feet, wrinkles, or sagging skin. Signs he was sure belonged to all 30-year-old women.

"I need some sleep." Cherri opened her car door then stood outside waiting. "Well, come on. We're not going to spend the night in your car. What would your neighbors think?" She half-smiled and closed her car door.

The girl in the restaurant seemed to have disappeared and was now replaced by this woman. Butch's door squeaked and he remembered the WD40 in his trunk. He'd have to take care of that tomorrow. Now all he wanted was sleep. Cherri walked beside him and averted making eye contact. They climbed the two flights of stairs in silence. Butch opened his very unkempt studio apartment and motioned Cherri in. "You can sleep on the couch. It sort of lets out. The bathroom is down the hall and you'll find sheets and pillows in the closet to your left. I'm sure you won't have trouble finding anything. Good-night."

"Thanks for rescuing me. I really mean it." For the first time Cherri smelt Butch's Old Spice and remembrance of her father floated through her mind.

"Good-night." Butch's long lanky body slumped as he walked toward his air mattress in the far corner.

Cherri grabbed a napkin from the coffee table and rubbed off the lipstick she had applied at Sears. She sank into the couch and ascended into dreamland.

Cherri awoke with the sun shining through the half-opened blue mini-blinds and with a headache that started at her temple and raced to the back of her head. She focused her eyes and found herself in a miniature apartment. All the doors stood open leading to a small bathroom and three closets. Black towels lay balled up on the bathroom floor; men's underwear, pants, and shoes were disarranged on top of a sunshine yellow beanbag chair; and dust, Cherri hated dust, was visual on top of what Cherri thought was a brown plastic coffee table. Her right hand went instantly to her temple as she smoothed the area hoping for relief. *I've got to remember the night.* She sat up and gazed around the room. *Butch. I only had one beer, or did I? Jack Daniel and Fitzgerald's.*

Cherri lunged for the bathroom. Her head lingered over the toilet for what seemed like hours. She gagged and heaved, but now nothing came up. The night reappeared between each retch. She felt his presence and forced herself not to look up. A hand now rubbed her untangling braids as he squatted beside her.

His voice softly soothed her. "Good morning. But I guess it's not such a good morning for you?"

Cherri compelled herself to look at him. A weak smile and a sigh escaped her lips. "Ah." Her eyes averted downwards.

"I'm, uh," She wiped tears from the corner of her eyes. "I need a few minutes, if you don't mine?"

"No problem." Butch closed the bathroom door as he left Cherri still on her knees.

Cherri slowly stood and looked at her haunting image in the mirror. Pulling her braids back, she found an elongated rubber band and arranged her store bought hair in a ponytail. She took a slightly used washcloth and applied cool water to her face. Scrubbing, she tried to remove all traces of her smudged mascara. Her bronzed skin now shrieked with images of red. Cherri opened the bathroom door and emerged herself into Butch's palace. Still a little shaky, embarrassed, and not sure of what her next move should be, she kept her eyes lowered.

"I seem to be asking you this a lot, but are you okay?" No smile escaped Butch's lips.

"Yeah, I'm fine. I, er, think I better be going now." She slowly walked toward his door.

"Cherri?"

"Yes." She turned, her heart pounded.

"Last night, you said you didn't have any place to go. Is that true?"

"Yes. I got the first eviction notice three weeks ago; apparently the mortgage hadn't been paid in some time. My husband," Cherri took a big breath trying not to cry, "took care of most of the bills, all of the bills, and the money. He took all of the money. I stayed, hoping for a miracle; that my husband would come back." Hesitation now penetrated Cherri's voice. "I guess I'll be going." Cherri slowly stepped closer to the door.

"You can stay." Butch's voice was barely a whisper escaping his lip.

Her heart escalated. She turned quickly to face him. "What?"

IN A BOTTLE

"I said, you may stay. At least until you find somewhere else. It's not very big, but you can stay. A few days."

"Thanks." Cherri's smile was back. "I'll clean and cook, and," Cherri stopped herself. "I don't know how to do anything else." She apologized, "I'm a married woman. That's all I was allowed to do for twelve years."

"My class starts in thirty minutes. I've got to be at work at 5:00 p.m. So, I won't be back until 1:30 a.m. I do have one luxury, cable TV, a perk for living here." Butch's slender muscular body stood next to Cherri as he tried to exit. "There's an extra key on top of the refrigerator."

"Thanks."

Their hand's touched momentarily as their eyes locked. "I'll see you later."

"Butch, Thanks, I really mean it."

"I've been there before, don't worry about it."

Before Cherri could ask what he meant, Butch was running down the stairs. Old Spice lingered in the air.

In the cramped area that housed the stove and refrigerator, Cherri found a compact washer and dryer. She gathered socks from under the sofa, clothes from off the beanbag, floor and mattress, and towels, sheets, and washcloths. She combined her clothes with Butch's and mindlessly washed. Butch's tee shirt freely fit her like a micro-mini dress. Cherri sat crossed-legged on the floor with remote in hand. She found reruns of <u>I Love Lucy</u> that took her mind off of real life. Cherri found peace and laughter and slept.

Butch found Cherri curled up on the floor, clenching the remote, volume blasting. He gently removed the remote from her clutching fingers and lowered the volume. She slept. He contemplated which would be more comfortable: spending hours on the hard floor or sleeping on his air mattress. As he lifted her, she clung to him like a sleeping child. Butch felt warm through his Homer Simpson tee shirt. The outline of her body was more than visible. He softly lowered her to his bed and covered her. Cherri slept. Butch spent the night on his sofa watching television with fleeting thoughts of the woman he met in his father's restaurant, of how their lives parallel each others. He dozed throughout the night and was finally sleeping when he felt the presence of someone standing over him.

"Are you sleeping?" Cherri's meek voice attempted to rouse him.

"Yes, what time is it?"

"3:30. I saw you moving and I thought you were awake."

"That's okay, what's wrong?"

Cherri didn't answer. Butch opened his eyes and as they adjusted to the darkness he saw the image of Cherri. "Is anything wrong?" He was trying to shake the daze from his mind. "Cherri?"

"No, I just wanted to talk."

"Can't it wait until morning?"

Cherri's nodded and returned to the corner. She wanted to sit, but the sofa was the only real furniture in the studio.

Butch rose and turned to face Cherri. She sat cross-legged staring in his direction. He could make out her large eyes and her full-round lips, the features he found most attractive. Against his better judgment, he joined her. He held her, and eventually, they both slept.

Cherri felt the warmth of Butch's body against hers and his breath on the nape of her neck. She removed his heavy arm and sat up. He slept soundly and only turned on his back. She gathered her clothes from the laundry basket and proceeded to his bathroom. Showered, she quickly dressed in wrinkled clothes. Butch still slept. She stole $50.00 from Butch's wallet, and making sure she had his extra key, exited.

Butch awakened to the illuminated dial of his alarm clock, 10:00 A.M., and the silence of his apartment. He listened for Cherri, but found no sign of her. He stood and surveyed his studio again. There was no evidence of life. Butch didn't have time to contemplate her absence. It was Saturday and he worked the lunch shift. He had one hour to get to work. Entering his bathroom, he smelt the slight scent of Old Spice. Not allowing himself to think, he quickly showered and departed for work.

In her Brentwood neighborhood all the houses were brick. She opened their customized mailbox her husband had commissioned. Cherri only took mail addressed to Mrs. David Bonbarsky. She never received important mail addressed to Cherri Jubilee Bonbarsky. She left obvious monthly bills, mortgage company threats, and junk mail. Two letters caught her attention, both from attorney offices: a thick letter from Dunbar and Dunbar, and a thin one from Smith, Carter and O'Riley. Worry lines crossed her face. She pocketed these two letters and a letter from her sister. Looking around Cherri saw no neighbors. She crept to her front door and skeptically gazed at her key. Her hand shook as she found the keyhole; she turned the lock and the door opened.

Homeless one less day.

Beer bottles carpeted the living room floor, stabbed pictures of her husband lined the couch, and her wedding band - Cherri bent to reach for her ring and stopped. Instead she sat on pictures of her husband. "Enmy, minny, miney, moe." Cherri chose the thin letter. The word "Eviction," made Cherri drop the letter. Using her finger as a letter-opener, Cherri opened the thicker parcel. Tears clouded her vision as she read DIVORCE. Cherri deposited the letter with the rest of the trash lining their dark gray carpet, grabbed her wedding band, and proceeded upstairs.

She opened her top dresser drawer and gathered a miniature ship in a bottle that she had helped build twelve years ago, her secret stash of cash, a crumpled up brown paper bag, and her small jewelry box. She gazed at her 2-carat diamond engagement ring that she was only allowed to wear on special occasions, and her oversized diamond and ruby earrings. She gathered VISA and Sears credit cards belonging to Mrs. David Bonbarsky - surely David would have cancelled them - lipstick, and along with her top drawer contents, placed them in her carry-on bag. She also placed two changes of normal clothes, make-up, shoes, and miniature stuffed animals: ten little bears and two snowmen collected on their yearly vacations. She walked her house from memory; she knew every square foot. Her house - the house she designed and David allowed her to build. Her purse lay open on the kitchen table. Cherri couldn't recall how she managed to travel to Fitzgerald's Thursday night.

IN A BOTTLE

The sound of the front door closing startled Cherri. She recognized David's voice. But the familiar high-pitched female voice caused her to glance through the partially opened kitchen door. Cherri caught her breath, grabbed her bags, and quickly rushed through the back door, leaving her keys in the living room. She walked the two blocks to the nearest bus stop and waited for the next downtown bus. Her mind raced. Marge's daughter, she could not believe David had left her for her best friend's daughter. Marge had recently gone through a divorce and left town to live with her mother, leaving her life and her daughter in Nashville. Curled up on the bench, she allowed herself to cry.

Homeless for real.

Downtown, Cherri found Barry's Pawnshop on 4th Avenue. She checked the payphones on each corner of the shop, but each proved empty. A homeless man stared at her for entering his domain. She pulled the door open and entered Barry's. A man ready for retirement stood behind the counter, "May I help you?"

Cherri opened her jewelry box and placed her custom made wedding band and 2-carat diamond engagement ring on the glass counter top. "How much?" She choked on her words.

The white-haired gentleman closely examined her rings, rising an eyebrow, he said "$1,000.00".

Cherri nodded. Even though she needed money, she hating taking the jeweler's unreasonable offer. Her exquisite wedding band and engagement ring were now part of her past. Street people, tourists, and business people stared at her. She walked with head down going nowhere, her cowboy boots clicking on the pavement. Cherri had aimlessly walked and now found herself in front of the Renaissance Hotel. The doorman opened the door and half-greeted her; instead of entering she asked him to hail a taxi.

The taxi stopped outside of Butch's building and Cherri gathered strength to continue her life. She was not sure why she had even bothered to come back, except to return the $50.00 she had "borrowed" that morning. Cherri's door opened and Butch stood with WD40 in one hand. She paid the cabdriver and gathered her belongings.

Butch said nothing.

Slowly she departed the cab and stood in front of Butch. He stared down at her, arms crossed, but Cherri thought she saw a slight smile. Silences lingered.

"I borrowed some money from you this morning." Cherri confessed. "I needed to get some things, but I didn't have..."

"One week."

"What?"

"I think one week is enough time for someone to get her life together. You can stay one week." Butch turned to go.

Cherri's mouth finally closed and she found a seat on the bottom step. *"Why did I bother to return?"* She whispered to herself.

"Why?" Butch stood over her.

She looked into the sun at the vision of Butch. She couldn't read his expression, but she felt his anger. For the first time in three days, she tried to think, to be honest to the person who cared for her when she was at her lowest. "I want to be here." Soberness awoke her. "This morning I felt real for the first time in months. I believed someone cared what happened to me."

Butch now shared her step. She leaned her head against his chest and inhaled his scent, her father's scent. He stroked her hair and planted a kiss on her forehead. She closed her eyes and let her life drain into him. He wrapped her in his arms.

"Would you do me a favor?" Butch whispered.

His voice brought her back to reality. "Yes."

"Next time you need money, would you ask first?"

"I promise." She smiled.

He still held her. "Do you have any plans?"

"I got a letter from my sister in Ohio. I think I talked to her when David first left. When I was last sober. I don't know how to do anything except cook and clean. She wants me to come stay with her. She's a financial planner and she thinks I'll be good at it. There's all kind of training. She never liked David. But to answer your question, I would like to take you up on your offer to stay, for a week. Really think things out; now that I'm sober. I can pay rent."

"That won't be necessary. I know what it's like being homeless when no one cares." He averted his eyes from Cherri as she looked up.

"You keep saying that. I've bared my soul to you, do you want to talk?"

"Maybe later. Matilda has gotten me dirty and I need a shower."

"Matilda?"

"My car. Come on. I'll flip you for the mattress?"

"We could share."

Butch only smiled and raced up the stairs with Cherri dragging her belongings behind her.

Cherri woke gasping for breath. For the first time all week, Butch had not awakened her before he left. The week had sped by and the only decision she wanted to make was to stay in Butch's world. She had grown comfortable in the small space of his apartment.

She cooked breakfast and dinner, washed dishes, did the laundry, cleaned bathroom and living space, and dusted. At first she used dishcloths to dust, but on the top shelf of his closet she found Butch's yellow-handle duster, feathers still wrapped in plastic with the $1.00 price tag on the handle. She also found a box labeled "Demons" containing old curled-up pictures and letters in envelopes addressed to "DAD" with the year in the upper left-hand corner. The envelopes were dated 1995 through 2004. She also found letters addressed to "MOM" for the same years; and one envelope addressed to her. Her letter was on purple stationary with hand painted swans in each corner. Her letter was dated week one 2005. *"Cherri, she's a little girl in a woman's body,"* as Cherri read the first few words guilt rushed through her. She shivered. She forced herself to put the letter aside. Instead she examined one of the pictures. On the back of one was 1994, "the end." They were family photographs where everyone's smile appeared frozen. Cherri told herself she was only exploring, but her guilt made her return the pictures and letters without going through them. When she was not cleaning, she watched reruns of old comedies and laughed into dreamland.

Tomorrow her week was up and Butch believed in promises kept. She had to make a decision. She did not have many options after going through the new set of divorce papers delivered to Butch's address for her to consider. Her husband left nothing to chance; he was now going to charge her with adultery and abandonment. She couldn't afford an attorney; so David had the power to paint any picture he wanted. He had invaded her privacy and enclosed a picture of her and Butch embraced outside the apartment complex. On the back of the photo he had written "insurance," but the offer of $24,000 did not seem to equal the twelve years she had given of her life. She would probably take the offer rather than fighting him and get nothing.

For the past twelve years, Cherri's real job had been taking care of David and making sure she was presentable to the elite. Now he possessed a new clone. *"I saved you from yourself and I am your life."* David had embedded these words in Cherri's head since she was eighteen and even had the inscription engraved on a gold bracelet he had given her for her nineteenth birthday. Her mother, oh how her mother had pushed her into the marriage. David had taught Cherri that everyone bent to money; even blood flowed thin when money was offered. Twelve years she had lived in David's bubble.

On her usual walk that morning, she had stopped by the corner store and bought bananas and apples and a home pregnancy test.

The lines turned positive.

Cherri read the instructions over a second time and prayed. But the plus sign only rendered her fears.

She was pregnant.

David had been obviously drunk their last time together. She had turned into his society doll and David had toasted the night away with champagne and Cherri with her usual cranberry juice. David did not allow her to drink. They started at David's favorite restaurant, Fitzgerald's, and then onto Panda's Bar. He was celebrating his move up to CEO/President in the

Company and she was celebrating having David's attention and affection after months of rejections.

The next morning David went to work and never returned. That afternoon, Bridget, his new secretary, used David's key to gain access to her home. Bridget handed Cherri a note and a list of clothes and personal items to collect for him. The note from David was very short, "My secretary will be collecting my things, stay out of her way. Don't call. I will be in touch when I need you." Cherri had attempted to call, but she was always informed he was in conference. After three days of calling and trying to lie by faking an emergency or disguising her voice, she gave up. Instead, she turned to the bottle.

For the first time in a week, Cherri bawled. So loudly, she did not hear Butch enter.

Cherri's body quivered with each sob. Butch sat down next to Cherri and wrapped her in his arms. He rocked her.

"Shhh....everything will be all right."

Cherri's body relaxed. Old Spice lingered faintly in her nostrils. Her wails grew quiet. Her breath became normal. She clung to the body holding her. Peace again entered her soul.

Butch finally released Cherri, drying her cheeks gently with his fingertips.

Cherri's wet eyes found comfort in Butch's and she found herself reaching for him.

Butch held her until she released him. Butch took the napkin from the Captain D's fish dinner he had brought for them and gently wiped the tears from Cherri's eyes and cheeks. Cherri blew her nose on the napkin.

"I need a drink." The words choked from Cherri's throat.

"We can't always feed our needs. You want to talk about it?" Butch still danced around asking Cherri to reveal personal information. He knew when Cherri wanted him to know, she would tell him. Besides, his life was not up for questions. No one could invade his world.

They danced with life every day, neither wishing to speak the words that opened the door that brought them to closeness.

"It, no." Cherri lowered her head avoiding those piercing gray eyes. "I didn't get a chance to cook dinner."

"I've told you, you don't have to cook. The place looks great, but that's not your job. Besides, you're my guest."

"Oh."

"Hey, it's Friday, do you want to go out? We could get something to eat or go to a movie?"

"You've already stopped by Captain D's."

"Okay, what about a movie? I'll let you pick." Butch was unconsciously playing with her hair.

"You don't have to work tonight?"

"No, I traded off. I'm tired, besides I feel guilty not spending time....not seeing to my guest's needs."

Cherri observed Butch's forehead to see if his worry lines appeared. Sure enough, his forehead crinkled. "I don't know. I planned on watching TV."

"Cherri, you've been cooped up all week. There's nothing outside that can harm you unless you give them the power."

"Can we go for a walk in the park?"

"It's too late, the park is closed."

"I just want to watch TV. I don't like movies."

"Okay. Whenever you're ready to talk." Butch retrieved his cold French fries and handed Cherri the bag containing three fish sandwiches and another bag of fries. "Here, eat something."

"I'm not hungry." Cherri hated fast food and the smell was making her nauseated.

"Suit yourself." Butch clicked on the television and found "Nash Bridges."

Cherri went to the kitchen and found an open outdated Diet 7-Up. She sipped, hoping the soda would calm her stomach.

"So, have you decided what to do with your life?" Butch half asked, he was zoned into his one luxury.

"Not really. I was thinking about getting a job. I've been reading the want ads. I called my sister today. She has a new live-in boyfriend and right now wouldn't be a good time. She calls it the 'boy-of-the-month' club. You know, seeing how many guys she can date in thirty days and out of that how many are worthy of living with. So far she's up to six live-ins in eight months."

"Do you share your sister's beliefs?"

"My sister is eight years older than me, runs her own financial empire, never been married, and plans to be artificial inseminated when she turns 40 with some genius sperm. So, no, I could never be my sister."

"You never want children?"

Cherri closed her eyes and took a deep breath; sipped her soda and wondered how she had brought the subject around to children. When she looked up, Butch was watching her. "What did you say?" Cherri tried to keep the calm in her voice.

"I just asked if you wanted kids?"

"Do you?"

"I'm not sure. I'm sure I don't want someone to have my life." Butch smiled. "But I think it would be nice to have unconditional love; at least for the first few years when your kids think you're superman."

"Do you want a boy or girl?"

"Doesn't matter. I take it you don't want a little one?"

"I'm not sure." Cherri rubbed her stomach. "Under the right circumstances." She whispered more to herself. "Would you like something to drink?"

"You don't have to wait on me."

"Why not? You wait on people all day, now it's your turn."

"Okay, chocolate milk."

"Coming right up." Cherri's hands trembled as she took the glass from the drying rack. She poured the milk without spilling and sat the container back in the refrigerator. She took another sip of her soda and went to join Butch on the sofa.

"Here you go."

"Thanks." Butch noticed the slight shake in Cherri's hand. "Are you all right?"

"Fine." She sank into the over-soft couch and Butch's weight brought her closer to him than she had planned. Cherri pretended to watch television. She smelled his Old Spice and calmed herself. She would have to find a new doctor Monday. David played golf with Dr. Mason, her regular doctor. She could see them now plotting to take her child. But did she really want this child? Not now, not David's child. Cherri hungered for a beer, just one. "Okay, why don't we go out for drinks?"

"I don't drink, remember?"

"I could drink and you could just get something." Cherri's voice rose as she tried to control her anxiety.

"Cherri, I'm not going to feed your habit. You're welcome to go alone or you could tell me what's bothering you. Telling someone your burden will lighten your spirit."

"Ha, like you." Her eyes widen.

"I don't have any problems. I have circumstances that life has dealt me and I have learned how to deal with them. I have locked my demons away."

"I don't know anything about you! What are your demons!?" She shouted.

Butch clicked off the remote. "You know enough. More then most." Butch's voice was still soft and calming. "Come on, I won't judge you."

"I'm, I'm," she swallowed hard, "I'm pregnant!" Cherri looked straight ahead, biting her lower lip, she didn't want to see Butch's reaction. After five minutes of silence, she glanced at him. "Well?"

Butch's eyes pierced her soul. "Do you feel better?"

She hated the serenity in his voice. "No."

"Do you have any plans?"

"No."

"Have you been to a doctor?"

"No. I don't have one."

"Okay, I think you need to see a doctor first."

"I'm late and I took the home pregnancy test. I am pregnant!" David's face appeared before her, but reality snapped her back. "I'm sorry, I didn't mean to shout at you."

"You did, but that's okay. You know you'll have to make some plans."

"Plans," Cherri's mind raced, surely he wasn't talking about abortion. "What kind of plans are you talking about?"

"What kind of life you plan on bringing your baby into? How are you going to support yourself? When are you going to tell your husband? Should I go on?"

"No. I don't want to think right now. I'll decide tomorrow."

Butch squeezed her shoulders. "Okay, just remember, I'm still your friend."

Cherri wanted to know how far friendship would carry them, but was afraid to ask. "Okay."

"You can stay a little longer. But, you have to make a life for yourself. I am not David. I don't need a maid."

Cherri smiled thinking of the day she entered his place.

Butch returned her smile, "Okay, my place was sort of disorganized and I thank you for all your efforts, but I can survive without a servant. Okay?"

"Yeah, right."

"Let me fix you something to eat. A diet soft drink is not nutritious. I'm sure we have some of your great leftovers in the refrigerator."

Before Cherri could answer, Butch was in the kitchen. She moved closer to where the sofa still held his warmth and essence.

After baked chicken, salad, and rolls, Cherri and Butch spent the night laughing at reruns of Gilligan's Island and Andy Griffith. They snuggled under Butch's tattered Winnie the Pooh blanket. Neither spoke. They slept in this position until morning light flickered in their eyes.

Cherri raced for the bathroom and threw up. Butch found Cherri on her knees. Wetting a washcloth, he applied the coolness to the nape of her neck. Bending down, he massaged her shoulders until the tightness released its hold on her.

Cherri sat back on her ankles and brought the washcloth to her forehead. "Thanks."

Butch knelt down beside her, "I think you need to see a doctor."

"It's Saturday."

"I have a friend. I pretty sure she'd see you today."

Cherri's eyes held disbelieve. She said nothing.

"Don't look at me that way. I met her at work. She's a regular. Dr. Demins."

"She's an obstetrician?"

"I think so. I have her card." Butch's long legs reached the kitchen table in two strides. He emptied the contents of his wallet and picked up the folded pink business card adorned with a pink kiss.

Cherri saw the blood floating in the commode that had come from within her. She flushed. She had also noticed spots in her underwear yesterday, but the blood was smaller than her pinky nail. Cherri slowly made her way into the kitchen and stood looking.

"Um, home phone number, cell phone number, lipstick. I think she wants to doctor on you."

Butch blushed.

"So, does she?"

"I wouldn't know. Would you like me to call her?

"No, I'm okay." Cherri wiped perspiration from her forehead, took two steps towards the sofa and collapsed.

Whiteness enfolded Cherri. She blinked and closed her eyes again. The slight beeping noise was continuous. She squinted. Butch sat in the corner, head down. Opening her eyes, images continued to become real and she realized she was in a hospital room. Her hand went instantly to her stomach and a small whimpering sound escaped.

"Cherri?" Butch stood by her side. "Cherri?"

Cherri forced her lips tight to keep the noise inside.

IN A BOTTLE

Butch's fingers gently caressed her forehead. "You're okay."

"What about the baby?"

Butch was silent too long. He reached for the call button.

"Oh, God, I killed it!" Cherri was pulling at tubing inserted in her arm, her arms flew wildly. "I killed it! I didn't want it! I killed it!"

Butch physically held her. "Shhh. You didn't kill your baby. It's just God's way."

Cherri quivered. Butch held her until the sobs stopped. Until her body grew limp with exhaustion. He softly laid her back. Tears still rolled down her cheeks, to her neck, and quietly onto her pillow.

The nurse returned with a sedative. Cherri lay quiet. She checked Cherri's IV and administered the tranquilizer. "That should calm her. I'm sorry for your loss." Said more to Butch then to Cherri.

Butch nodded. Cherri's eyes fluttered and sleep soon invaded her world. Butch reluctantly dialed Fitzgerald's.

"Fitzgerald's."

Butch paused.

"You've reached Fitzgerald's. May I help you?"

"Dad?"

"Yes, Jason?"

"I can't come in for my shift today. A friend of mine is in the hospital."

"Is there anything you can do for them? Give blood? Give a kidney?"

"No."

"Did you win the lottery?"

"No."

"Then I expect you in as scheduled."

Before Butch could answer, his father hung up. Butch already knew he would not leave Cherri. Instead, he dialed Mary Ellen to see if she could cover for him at Fitzgerald's.

"Mr. Fitzgerald's not going to be too happy with you Butch. He raised hell when we switched Friday."

"I know. But I can't leave right now. I have to be sure she's okay. I know the doctor say she's fine, but they don't know her."

"Sounds like you've falling."

"Can you just do me this favor? I promise the next time you need off."

"Okay, okay, he's your father."

"Thanks, Mary Ellen."

"Butch?"

"Yeah?"

"Don't get involved too much. She sounds like she has a lot of problems to deal with. I know how ex's are."

"I'm okay. She's just a friend."

"Yeah."

"Thanks again."

"You're welcome, Butch."

Butch sat down on the edge of the chair and watched Cherri. She slept. He took a piece of paper from the drawer of the table and composed a letter to his father.

"November, 2005

Dad:

Compassion doesn't exist in your world. I never ask you for favors. You wouldn't know how to love or care if your life depended on it. You left Mom, not the other way around. Yes, she physically left you, but mentally you had vanished two years before. Becoming a "big" businessman in the eyes of society was your goal, and we ceased to be important. I guess I should thank you for giving me a job, but I won't...."

IN A BOTTLE

◈

"Butch?"

Butch shifted the paper behind him as he caught Cherri glancing at him, "Cherri, how do you feel?"

"My head hurts, and my throat's dry."

"I'll get you some water."

"What happened? Where am I?" Cherri closed her eyes then opened them. Butch stood beside her.

"Here's your water. Can you lift up a little?"

Cherri tried to sit up, but could only move her head. "I don't think so. I feel like I'm floating."

"Let me adjust your bed. The doctor said you can go home tomorrow."

"Your doctor?"

"Yes."

"I lost my baby?"

"Dr. Demins said there was nothing that could have been done." Butch looked away.

"I killed her. I decided I didn't want to have David's child and I killed her."

Butch moisten a washcloth and applied it to her head. "No, you didn't do anything."

"I saw the blood. I should have gone to a doctor then."

"It wouldn't have made a difference. You can have more children."

"Typical man's answer. What makes you think I want more children?"

"I'm sorry."

Cherri's eyes were glazed and she fought the tears. She wanted to scream, but was too tired. "I'm going to sleep. Why don't you go home? I don't need you."

"That's fine." Butch took his seat and began writing again.

Cherri glanced at him. "What are you writing?"

"Nothing."

"Is it for your collection in your closet?" Cherri words flowed out and she regretted diving into his private world.

"So you found my demons?"

"Yes, but I didn't read any of them?"

"Not even the one to you?"

"Not really."

"When we go home, you can read it. I wrote it the night we met. It's how I cope with the world. Who knows? One day I'll write my memoirs."

"Does it help? Writing I mean."

"Sometimes. Other times I'm just blowing off steam. I write fast and don't correct the mistakes. You could say, it calms me."

Cherri had drifted back to sleep. Butch covered her, sat down to continue his letter, and dozed off. The ringing phone startled Butch. Cherri slept on.

"Hello."

"Butch, it's Mary Ellen. You father won't let me work for you. He says if you're not here in thirty minutes, you can kiss your job good-bye. If I was you, I'll get down here."

"Thanks, but I'm not coming. I can get another job. Waiters are a dime a dozen. I'm not bowing this time. Tell him to go kiss his...."

"Butch, I'm going home. You can deliver your own message. I can't afford to get fired. He's already written me up for insubordination. One more and I'm out the door."

"I'm sorry, Mary Ellen. I'll take care of my father tomorrow. Right now I'm needed here. Thanks for trying to help."

"Butch, do me a favor and don't do anything foolish."

"I won't. Thanks again."

Cherri still slept and Butch fought the desire to crawl next to her, to protect her. Instead, he stretched out in the chair and tried to sleep - his father on his mind.

Butch awakened to the touch of hands on his shoulder and a soft voice whispering his name.

"Dr. Demins?" Butch blinked the sleep out of his eyes.

"Morning. You should have gone home. You would have been more comfortable."

"I didn't want her to wake up alone." Instead of looking at Dr. Demins, Butch stared straight at nothing.

"I see."

"How is she?"

"Physically, she's fine. She can go home today." Dr. Demins looked over at Cherri. "Too bad she didn't come in earlier, we might have been able to save her baby."

"Yeah."

"I see she has your last name. Is she a relative?"

"My sister." He turned his head to advert his eyes from the doctor.

"Really? Are you going to be working tonight?"

Butch could feel Dr. Demins' eyes on him, but he didn't look up. A chill moved slowly through his body and caused an involuntary shiver. He could only nod.

"I'll see you there."

Butch thought Dr. Demins walk was slowed. She paused at the door, but continued without speaking. Butch wiped the perspiration off his forehead and slowed his breathing. He felt Cherri looking at him. "Good morning."

"I heard the doctor. It was my fault. My baby died because of me."

"You need to put this behind you. You can't change the past, Cherri. The doctor said you can go home today."

"I don't have a home." Cherri laid back and closed her eyes.

Butch moved closer to Cherri's side. "I know my place isn't quite a real home, but my invitation is still open. I'll take you home with me."

Cherri didn't answer.

"Come on, you can have the mattress. I'll give you one of my world famous massages. I promise it will take all your worries away." Butch thought he saw the beginning of a smile. He took Cherri's hand and played with the cut on her thumb. "I promise you," he paused, "that life has a way of healing all your hurts." He kissed her thumb.

Tears rolled down Cherri's cheeks. Butch sat down and held her. They gently rocked. Cherri lifted her head from his shoulder and kissed his cheek.

Their eyes locked. Slowly they came closer together and kissed. Long, soft, and passionate. When they parted, their eyes held them together, finally their breath slowed and both looked away. Butch got up and looked out the window at downtown Nashville. Cherri closed her eyes.

"Good Morning, I'm Isabella." The door slammed open and Cherri jumped. "Are we ready for breakfast?" The nurse placed a breakfast tray down and removed the lid. "So, how do you feel, Ms. Fitzgerald?"

Cherri's eyes widened and she glanced at Butch. "Fine."

"Good. When you finish your breakfast, you can go home."

"I'm not hungry."

"Doctor's orders. Why don't you see if you can get a little down?" Isabella adjusted Cherri's bed and tray, then left.

"Ms. Fitzgerald?"

"I didn't know if your last name was Jubilee. Plus they needed consent from a relative."

"That's right, I'm your?"

"Sister."

"Sister?"

"Yes." Butch finally faced Cherri. "I'm sorry about the kiss. I don't..."

"As I recall, I kissed you and I'm in no way sorry."

Butch smiled and slowly moved closer to her bed. He picked up the spoon and fed her oatmeal.

"I hate oatmeal."

"Okay." Butch brought the next spoonful of oatmeal and Cherri's round lips parted. "The right touch makes everything taste delicious." Butch found his heart beating fast, but he calmed himself and his maleness.

After half a bowl of oatmeal, two strips of bacon, and two scrambled eggs, Cherri pushed the spoon away. "I can't"

"Okay, you did good. I'll get the nurse to help you get ready."

Before Cherri could object, Butch's long legs were through the door. Outside, Butch leaned against the wall and sighed. His emotions had never been so intense and confused. He went to the nurse's station and told Isabella Cherri was ready. Butch then went for fresh air. Outside he inhaled a long, deep breath.

He craved a cigarette; a habit he had conquered three years ago. The cool air washed his face; he stretched, and found a bench to steal a few moments of thoughtful peace. He watched people with their intense facial looks absorbed in their own pain. He tried to pray. He labored to remember his early years when life was simple and he had a real family. Nothing appeared. Twenty minutes passed and Butch departed to see if Cherri was ready.

Cherri sat on the side of the bed as Isabella helped her into a wheelchair.

"That's right, don't rush." Isabella coached her.

Butch watched as Cherri did a slow dance with pain. Her face was stern, but her eyes held agony. Butch wasn't sure if her suffering was physical.

"Okay. Mr. Fitzgerald, why don't you get your car and wait for us out front."

"Yes, ma'am."

"Ms. Fitzgerald and I will be right there." She patted Cherri on the shoulder.

"Butch!?"

Butch stopped at the sound of Cherri's voice.

"Thank you."

Butch only nodded and departed.

On the twenty-five minute ride home, neither found reason to speak. Cherri looked out the window. Her hand rested on her stomach. Butch drove slower then the speed limit and directed his attention on the morning traffic.

Butch pulled into the reserved handicapped parking space next to his stairwell. "Let me get your door."

Cherri found the courage to smile. The pain pill that Isabella had given her was finally beginning to work. She nodded at Butch.

Butch opened Cherri's door and gently pulled her out. "Steady now. I have to move my car before we go up. Mr. Smith might need his spot before I get back. I'll help you over to the stairs."

"No, I can wait here."

"Okay."

Cherri watched as Butch backed his car into the parking spot directly behind Mr. Smith's reserved spot. Life had definitely taken a turn for the worst. She had not only lost her home, her husband, and her normal life, but now the child that she did not feel she had wanted. She felt empty. Cherri watched as the tall, too young, yet too lovable man crossed to assist her. She wondered what had possessed her to kiss him.

"Ready?"

"You don't have to go to all this fuss. I can manage by myself."

"Cherri, I don't have time to argue with you."

Cherri didn't have time to object before she was being lifted into his arms. Butch carried her up the stairs. She felt weightless and safe. Butch deposited her by the door and retrieved his keys.

"I have to go to work at 10:30, but first I want to get you settled."

"But..."

"Cherri, Dr. Demins wants you to rest. Your body needs time to heal. Just give it a couple of days and then I'll let you do whatever you want. Okay?"

Cherri found herself smiling, "Okay. You know, you're nothing like David."

"I'll take that as a compliment. Now, get undressed and get in bed. I'm going to fix you something to eat for later." Butch was in the kitchen before Cherri had a chance to object. "Let's see, a pitcher of water, an apple, ah peanut butter and crackers. I'll pick something up on my way home tonight."

Butch returned with a tray to the nude Cherri. He sat the tray down and pulled a tee shirt from the dresser. "You can wear this. You wouldn't want to get cold." Butch held the tee shirt out to Cherri and inhaled the whole of her.

Cherri advanced closer. "Thanks." She did a slow dance into the tee shirt. "Do you have to go to work?"

Butch wasn't sure whom he was dealing with: the girl he had first met or the woman he was falling for. "Unfortunately, yes. I'm only working the lunch shift. I'll be back before you know it." He swallowed hard.

"Promise?" Cherri felt woozy; the medication was affecting her, freeing her.

"Promise. Keep the phone near you in case anything happens. Call me, okay?"

"I promise."

"Here's the remote. Remember you need to rest." Butch felt hot. The blood rushed to his face. "I'll be back soon." Butch bolted from his apartment with the image of Cherri's body playing in his mind.

Cherri settled on the mattress and turned on the television. She thought about calling David, but she couldn't find a reason. She had gotten another notice from David's attorney that David was still willing to give her $24,000 for a quick no-fault divorce. If not, the amended decree would be filed containing the charge of adultery and nothing would be offered. The package had also contained another photo of Butch and her embraced in Butch's apartment with the threat that there were more photos. She had three days before the divorce papers would be filed in court. She signed the no-fault agreement and returned it to the self-addressed envelope. She kissed the photo and put it on the plastic night stand. Her thoughts returned to David and Marge's daughter Phyllis. Eighteen. She soon descended into a restless sleep. Cherri could hear the screaming, but could not make out the television show. She was being shaken. Her voice screamed. Someone - David? - was purring her name. She felt warmth.

"Shhh..I'm here. You're okay." Butch held Cherri in his arms until she ceased trembling. He rubbed her hair and cooed her like a baby.

Cherri opened her eyes to find herself in Butch's arms. "What happened?"

"You were having a nightmare. Are you all right?"

Cherri inhaled Old Spice, "Yeah, I'm okay. What time is it?"

"11:30."

"I thought you had to work or is it later then I think?"

"No it's still morning. I have some time off. Daddy suspended me for a week. Said he was being merciful, he only wanted to teach me a lesson this time." Butch half smiled and released his hold on Cherri. "Are you sure you're okay?"

Cherri felt flushed. "It was just a nightmare." She leaned against the wall and tried to focus on the moment. "What happened?"

"Nothing much. You can read it when I write my memoirs." He winked at Cherri. "I brought you something?"

"You can't afford to be buying me things!"

"Easy now, don't get upset, it's just lunch. You are hungry?"

Cherri didn't want to admit it, but her stomach was rumbling. "Just a little."

"Okay. We have Big Macs." Butch held up the McDonald's sack.

Cherri frowned.

"And," Butch smiled and lifted a white take-out box, "for the beautiful lady, filet mignon, medium, with baked potato, and roasted vegetables from Fitzgerald's."

"How did you..."

"I placed the order with Mary Ellen before I checked in. She slipped it out of the kitchen for me when Daddy wasn't looking. She's a good friend."

"But how did you know my favorite?"

"Well," Butch sat Cherri's food on the tray and opened it. "I finally remembered your husband. The face was always there, but placing it with the right man."

"You remember David?"

"He didn't tip very well."

Cherri smiled, "No. He doesn't believe in giving servants more then he would give God."

"Good thing God doesn't need the money." Butch grinned.

For the first time in days, Cherri laughed.

"Come on eat before your food gets cold." Butch had unwrapped his Big Mac and with one bite devoured half the sandwich.

Cherri inhaled. She took one bite and savored the taste. "Um. Real food." Cherri's smile faded. "Butch?"

"Uh huh."

"Are you going to be okay? Money wise, I mean."

"Don't worry. My Dad will probably call me first. I'm the only one willing to work a double on the weekend. Besides, I'd rather spend time with you. I haven't been a very good host. I was always running off to work or school. You know, we can exercise demons together." He winked at Cherri.

"Okay, David and your Dad. You'll have to teach me."

"I'll be glad to teach you anything."

For a moment their eyes locked. Butch looked away and continued eating. Silence fell between them. Butch turned on the television and relaxed beside Cherri.

Cherri ate her food feeling the warmth from Butch's body. Her heart raced as she remembered the kiss. "Butch?"

"Uh huh?"

"What's going to happen to us?"

"What do you mean?"

"You know," Cherri hesitated, "the kiss." She searched Butch's eyes for an answer.

"I don't know."

Cherri looked away.

"First," Butch's voice was soft, "I think you have to decide what you want. You have to stop depending on others to make decisions in your life. David played a mental game with you. You were his prisoner."

Cherri started laughing, "I can't believe you're saying this. I was his wife, not his prisoner."

"Cherri there are all kinds of abuse. And you were abused."

"Stop it! You don't know anything about me!" Her mouth pouted and she looked into Butch's eyes. "You weren't there. I did good. I really tried hard to be a good wife." Cherri wiped tears away.

"You were a better wife then he deserved. I've known plenty of Davids in my life. You're lucky you got out when you did. You're lucky he found someone else. You now have your freedom."

"But I don't know what to do." As hard as she tried, the sobs came.

Butch let her cry without comforting her.

After she had some control, Cherri handed Butch an envelope. "Would you mail this for me?"

Butch glanced at the address, "Sure."

"I don't like...," she shook her head and wiped her nose with her hand. "I want to get some sleep now."

Butch took a napkin and wiped her tears away. Cherri laid down, fetus position, and closed her eyes. Butch covered her and ascended to the sofa.

Cherri slept restlessly until dawn. Her body ached and her head hurt as she sat up. Butch's head slumbered off the end of the sofa. Cherri heard his soft breath wheezing. *I have to think*. Cherri closed her eyes and tried to image her future. Blackness existed before her. She nodded up and down thinking this would bring a forecast. Nothing. *I don't know how to think*.

Butch touched her arm and Cherri jumped. "Are you all right?"

IN A BOTTLE

Cherri opened her eyes to find Butch lending over her. "Yes. I was just thinking."

"Look, Cherri, I'm sorry about yesterday. I had no right to tell you about your life or what you should do. You're welcome to stay here until you decide, but you have to make some effort to continue your life. You can't hide out here. Okay?"

"Okay. But what if I can't."

"Can't what?"

"Can't make any decisions about the future."

Butch took a seat next to Cherri. "Okay. You have to support yourself."

"I know."

"And I don't mean to pry, but are you getting what you deserve in the divorce?"

"He made me an offer." Cherri lower her head and whispered, "$24,000."

"Do you feel that's a fair offer?"

"Under the circumstances, yes. I signed it already and you mailed it." Cherri played with her toes, "I'm letting go of the past."

Butch looked away, but keep his voice calm. "That's good. I'm sure you have a reason for settling for less then you've put into the marriage and if this helps you to move on, then that's good."

"I've never worked. I graduated high school one day and was married the next. David gave me everything. He was twenty-six, handsome, and needed a wife."

"Needed?"

"Yeah." She finally looked up, "His old man died and David would get all the money if he married a virgin within 48 hours of the death. Me."

"You?"

"Yeah, me. My mom cleaned house for them for fifteen years, and I would go along whenever school was out. Then sometimes when they had a party, they let me help. His father was always nice to me. He was always telling my mom that someday I would make some man a good wife, a dutiful wife. And whenever David saw me, he would wink. I fantasized about being with him. You know, being his girl friend." Cherri stared straight ahead as if in a trance. "When his father died, David told my Mom that he wanted to marry me, provided I was a virgin."

"And were you?"

A soft laugh escaped her lips, "Yes. I never had a real boyfriend. I had other problems, but boys weren't one of them. We were from the wrong side, if you know what I mean. Anyway, at first my Mom said I was too young, but then David offered her money. I overheard their conversation. He read her the Will. After that, I was married the next day. My Mom told me that I was about to become a princess. As poor as we were, I was about to be rich. She painted this glamorous picture of my future. None of it came true. Except, I did have all the booze I wanted, all the clothes he approved, and I was only poor in reality. I still cleaned his house." Cherri looked at Butch and continued, "I was happy at first..." Cherri swallowed, "for a few months I was Mrs. David Bonbarsky. I admit I was sort of stupid believing he was marrying me for anything except the money. I would still be with him today. I don't love David; I just need him to survive." Cherri bit her bottom lip.

Butch looked into her sad brown eyes, "What happened to your Mom?"

IN A BOTTLE

Cherri shook her head as tears slide from the corner of her eyes, "She brought a new car, a Cadillac. We always dreamed of visiting New York. We'd talked about how we were going to visit Broadway and shop on Fifth Avenue. So, she left, without me, a week after the wedding and an eighteen wheeler hit her head on. The police said she crossed the centerline. She was dead. Nothing anyone could do."

"I'm sorry."

"All her money went back to David, since I was his wife."

Butch shook his head.

"My father left when I was sixteen and my sister had already moved out. My father told me, I was almost grown and could take care of myself. He left one morning and never came back. Well, it's taken me thirty years to realize that life just isn't fair. Is it?"

"No. But..."

"Now, I have nothing. Well, I will have $24,000. That's something. Probably more then he gave my Mom."

"Cherri, I can't make you any promises, but somewhere in all this, there's... you've been given a new beginning. And you have to make the most of it. Just because you've never worked, doesn't mean you can't. There's a whole world out there that you've never experienced. You could go to school. Your sister's made it, and the world, well, you can't just crawl up and die. David probably thinks you will."

Cherri beheld Butch, "You know, I couldn't have made it this far without you. Thank you."

Butch found himself blushing, "Are you hungry?" His stomach rumbled.

Cherri's smiled, "Not really."

"Not really, that means you might be when we go out to get something." Butch was on his feet and pulling Cherri into his arms. "Come on, I'll draw you a warm bubble bath."

"That sounds okay."

"Just okay. Let's see, I'll..."

"Let me choose the place."

"Deal." Butch left Cherri and faded into the bathroom.

Cherri soon heard water running. She smiled. Somehow telling Butch her past had freed her. A weight had lifted off her shoulders and she could really smile. She unpacked her bag and pulled out a sundress she had balled up inside a paper bag. Yellow, she had begged David to let her buy it. He had consented since they were in the Bahamas and everyone dressed lively, but she was supposed to dispose of the sundress before they returned home. Instead she had put it in a bag and stuck it in her top drawer. She went to the kitchen and ironed the wrinkles away.

"Your bath is ready." Butch stood before her shirtless.

She glanced up but then took a longer look. She liked what she saw, but quickly adverted her eyes downward. "Thanks." She hung her dress on a hanger and put the backless sundress across the kitchen table. Butch now stood before her.

"Nice dress."

"You sound like you're shocked that I own normal clothes."

"I didn't say that." Butch was now beside her.

"Yeah, but your expression gave you away."

"Fair enough. I bet it will look better on you than on my table."

Cherri laughed. "I'm going to take my bath."

"You know, you have a beautiful laugh?"

She scooted past him and locked the bathroom door.

IN A BOTTLE

Cherri stood and dripped. She patted her body dry and realized she only had her towel to cover up. But it wasn't like Butch had not seen her body before. And that was her problem. She couldn't read his thoughts. Butch simply gave her something to cover herself with; none of the normal male behavior she was accustomed to. David would attack her whether he wanted her or to teach her one of his many lessons on his meaning of life and a woman's place. She was his wife and David could, would, and always did make love, screw her whenever he was in the mood. Cherri sat on the side of the tub and massaged the cocoa butter lotion that had appeared from nowhere, into her toes, legs, arms, her entirety. The scent relaxed her. She knew she had to make decisions, but she only wanted to live in the moment. And Butch was the moment. By the sink, was a sample bottle of Givenchy Organza with a note, "This smells better." She had only meant to spray the Old Spice into the air; to pretend she was not alone. That her father still loved her. That Butch could love her.

Cherri glanced at herself in the mirror. The eyes staring back were only hers. Cherri took another small round pain pill. She brushed her now unbraided hair to make it respectfully straight. She wrapped the damp towel around her; it almost fit, and emerged.

In the living area, she stopped. Butch watched television and slightly tilted his head towards her. He didn't speak. Cherri continued to the kitchen and dropped the towel. She could feel Butch's eyes upon her. She slowly slipped into her sundress then turned to face Butch. He watched.

"Do I look okay?"

Butch's lips contained a smirk, he glanced down. When his head lifted, the half smile was gone. "You should know that you are very beautiful. So, where am I taking you?"

"I've always wanted to go somewhere that's not so ritzy. Red Lobster?"

"Red Lobster is fine."

Cherri extended her hand to the seated Butch.

"Thank you." He stood close to Cherri. "You smell like my favor flower."

"And what kind of flower is that?"

"I'll tell you later." He kissed her softly on the lips. Cherri felt lightheaded. He quickly released her.

"Butch?"

"Yes."

Cherri reached up and touched his cheek with the back of her hand. She made him look into her eyes before she continued, "Can I stay with you?"

"Cherri," He looked away, "Let's just go get something to eat." His long legs striding for the door.

Cherri stood still. Her voice fluttered, "Butch, I need an answer."

He turned to face Cherri.

Cherri continued slowly, "I've bared my secrets to you. I've never told anyone before. Not even the wives of David's friends, I always pretended everything was okay. But I guess they did too. But you, you're, I don't know, I get these mixed signals from you. One minute I'm in your arms and the next I'm held at arm's length."

"You're too vulnerable right now. You need space to decide what you're going to do with your life." Butch advanced towards Cherri. "Look, I'm sorry."

"Would you stop being sorry!? I haven't loved my husband in years. I just never let myself stop the pretences. I couldn't. If he hadn't left me, I would still be there pretending I was in love and that his love, his abuse," she smiled, "was what all marriages were. You're only 21. God, 21." Cherri sat down on the sofa and stared at Butch. "I'm 30." Cherri closed her eyes and lowered her head. "I never think I'm getting old until I hear my age."

Butch crouched next to Cherri. "You are a lot younger then your age and I am older then mine, so that makes us equal."

"Butch, when you kiss me, what do you feel?" She found herself looking in his steal gray eyes for answers.

"Feel." He sat beside her, "My feelings are mixed. I know that you haven't resolved your situation yet, but I also know that I care about you. Love takes a long time to come for me. I haven't loved since I was fifteen."

"What happened at fifteen?"

"My mother left."

Cherri extended her hand to touch Butch's cheek, but changed her mind. "I'm sorry."

"She had to."

"You keep saying that."

"I've already filed away the details."

"I know, your box."

"If it would make you feel better, one day while I'm at work, you can read all of the letters."

"I don't think I want to. When you're ready, I'll listen." She squeezed his hand. "You know, I think I'm getting hungry now."

"Cherri?"

"Yes."

"I think I could love you."

"And I promise I'd never do anything to intentionally hurt you. I may not know what I want to do with my life, but I do know how to feel. I've run the gambit on feelings. Why don't we just be friends for now. I could use a good friend and something to eat."

"Okay." Butch rose and helped Cherri to her feet. He kissed her on her forehead, "Thank you."

Cherri held him. The warmth of his body penetrated her. She clung tighter as if life depended on them staying connected.

Butch lifted her, carried her to his bed, and slowly undressed her, admiring every crevice of her body.

For the first time, Cherri made love.

Morning came and they slept.

Butch woke first. He got up and put coffee on. He went to his closet and pulled down the box. Sorting through his letters, he began to read the ones addressed to his mother, then his father. Hours passed and he still read.

Cherri found Butch huddled in his closet reading, tears silently streaming down his cheeks. The box was empty except for one letter addressed to her. Butch picked up the letter and handed it to her. Cherri took the letter and tossed it back in the box.

"I'm not in the box." She took Butch's hand and helped him up. "Are you all right?"

"I was exorcising my demons." He wiped his cheeks and marched for the kitchen. "I made coffee. Do you want some?"

"No." She grabbed Butch's robe and covered herself. "Last night was beautiful."

Butch kept stirring his coffee. Finally, he turned to face her. "I don't know where this puts us now."

IN A BOTTLE

"Two people searching for their place in each other life. You don't have to feel obligated to me." Cherri stood in the middle of the living area looking at Butch.

"No, I didn't mean...I'm sorry, I've got to get some air." Butch was outside before Cherri could speak.

Cherri sat on the couch and cried. She gathered her thoughts and went to Butch's box. Sitting on the floor, she put the letters in order by date, then she read every word. Cherri cried for Butch.

Butch found her in a fetal position on the floor covered in his letters. He held her. Kissed her tears. And cuddled her.

"I didn't mean to walk out on you."

Cherri pushed away from his embrace. "I read your letters."

"I know."

"I wish I could take all your hurt and put the pain in a bottle and make it sail away." Cherri noticed the tears in the corner of his eyes. "Having the letters here just makes the hurt more prevalent." Cherri selected her words carefully, "Maybe you should throw these away or burn them."

Butch blinked and caught a tear, "I thought about mailing them." He faintly laughed. "I'll never really understood why she left me with him."

"I can't make excuses for her. At least my mother pretended to love me. Do you want me to get rid of them for you?"

"No. I graduate this Spring and then I'm starting on my memoirs." Butch stood, "Come on?" He extended his hand and lifted Cherri up. "We never made it to dinner. Do you want breakfast? Ella's Café around the corner has great omelets."

"Are you going to be a writer?"

"No. Hopefully, a computer technician."

"Not business?"

"No, I've been interning with Dell and I'm hoping a slot will open soon. You know, I was serious about you going back to school."

"Where did you go?"

"What?"

"When you left earlier, where did you go?"

"Just for a ride. When I was sixteen, he tossed me the keys to Mom's old car. It had been sitting in the garage for over a year. I finally made the engine purr and I left. I was free. I thought I was free."

Cherri wanted to bring Butch back to the present, "I'll go to breakfast, if you make me a promise."

"What?"

"That you'll never leave me in the middle of a conversation again. I felt empty." Cherri's mind raced over the times David had walked out on her, telling her, her opinion did not matter.

Butch thought for a second, "I am sorry and I promise to try to never make that mistake again."

"I guess I'll have to accept that. You know, I feel like cooking. I'll make you one of my omelets and you can compare."

"Only if this isn't an attempt to avoid the world."

"No, of course not. After we eat, I'll go anywhere you want."

"Okay. I think I need a cold, I mean hot shower. After we eat, we can go to a movie later."

"Sure." Cherri entered the kitchen: her world.

Butch appeared wrapped in a towel, wet tossed black hair, and a slight radiance to his body: baby oil. Cherri stared at his body: his hard abs, strong long muscular legs, and broad chest. Her mind drifted to last night.

"I hope you like what you see." Butch's broad smile broke her thoughts.

Cherri blushed. "I made you a western omelet. I hope you like it."

"Cherri, do you like what you see?"

"Yes, of course."

Butch came and hugged her. Her cheek felt the moisture of his skin. He sat and pulled her into his lap.

"I promise to never lie to you." Butch was holding Cherri close. "And to allow myself to express the feelings that my heart proclaims. But you have to do the same. I'm not going to force you to do anything that you don't want when it involves us. I won't pick out your clothes."

"But how did you know?"

"You looked like all the other patrons, remember?"

"That seems so long ago now. Like I woke up from a nightmare."

"I will force you to make a decision about your future."

"Butch, tell me what to do. Please?"

"I can't do that."

Cherri tried to free herself from Butch's hold, but he wouldn't let go.

"Think back. Before you got married, what did you want to do?"

Cherri sighed. "I wanted to go to New York."

"We'll go. What else?"

Cherri was silent for several minutes, "Something with kids." A sob caught in her throat and she felt her stomach. "Maybe a teacher."

"Then teach."

"I'm too old. I'll be thirty-four when I graduate."

"Stop thinking of yourself as old."

The firmness in his voice caught her off guard and she stiffen and relaxed in the same moment. Cherri nodded.

Butch kissed her forehead. "You know you have to write out a plan."

"Why?"

"Commit it to paper and you will believe. Put each step down. Don't worry, I'll help you."

"You really think I could teach?"

"If you want it and you believe, yes."

"Okay." Cherri reached and picked up a purple gel pen and black paper from Butch's plastic coffee table. "What's step one?"

"That's easy. Apply to Vanderbilt?"

"Vanderbilt!?" Cherri rolled her eyes.

"Stop that. Write. We'll submit your application for the fall term. There's lots of paperwork. Come on?" Butch picked Cherri up from his lap, grabbed his black jeans, and a wrinkled Homer Simpson tee shirt.

"Where are you going?"

He was dressed. "We're going to the library. We'll need to do research on what type of grants you can apply for."

"Don't you want your breakfast first?"

Butch smiled, "Sure."

"Your omelet is probably cold."

Butch took a seat at the table and poured ketchup on his food. Cherri stared.

He took one bite, "Delicious."

"How can you tell?"

"I said delicious. Keep working on your plan. Put finish dates on each major project."

Cherri's hand shook. "I don't know what else to put down."

Butch put his fork down and joined her on the couch. "That's okay." He took the paper away from her. "When you complete step one then the rest will follow." He squeezed her shoulders. "I'll hopefully know about Dell next week. I'll work nights at Fitzgerald's and days at Dell. We'll make it."

"We?"

"I do love you."

"You really do?"

"Really."

"Then would it be okay if I take some of my money and buy a bed?" Cherri felt herself going flush.

"I tell you what," Butch kissed her nose, "we can pick one out just as soon as we finish at the library."

Butch tired to rise, but Cherri held him down, "What if I don't make it? What if I fail?"

"Then we'll have to go to plan B."

"Plan B? What's plan B?"

"You'll know when you get there. Now come on?" Butch raced for the door.

Cherri followed. As she slammed the door, her ship in the bottle toppled to the floor.

SOCIETY THIN

Miranda sniffed her chocolate chap stick that resided on her night stand and called it breakfast. She felt nauseated when she thought of her sit-ups, but she snaked her way to the floor and religiously did her 110, if you're better than the rest you'll do your best, crunches to begin her day.

Now for the truth - weigh in. Miranda closed her eyes, stood naked, and said a small prayer, "Please, please, let the numbers be smaller."

Inhaling, Miranda stepped on her clear glass digital scale; half opened her eyes then looked down. Her shoulders sagged and her gut knotted. Swallowing, she held back tears and turned on her shower. The steam from her shower permeated her skin and she sweated. She loved the feel of hot hot water. Sweat poured off her forehead. For twenty minutes she endured the almost scalding baptism.

Miranda thought she was not society thin. At 5 feet 2 she weighed 100 pounds. In Miranda's mind lived her demons. Over the years, Miranda had lost over 65 pounds, but it never registered in her head that she was finally among the thin – not even from size 16 to 0 meant thin to her; only the number on the scale mattered.

For lunch, Miranda packed a can of Mocha Slimmer and a diet cream soda. She still craved chocolate and even though her cycle hadn't been regular in over a year, the cravings came and took her. Then she ran. She tried to out run her desire for solid food, her ten extra pounds that had attached itself to her rear end, and from the voices inside her head that chilled her from childhood calling her "fatty Matty, fat soul, fat, fat, fat, fat". Her mind taunted her that her body was vulgarly out of shape, grossly obese. When she looked in the mirror, all she saw were her "bulging" stomach, her "non-existence" hips, her flabby arms, and her watermelon thighs. Nothing Miranda did disrobed her of her mind's vision of her body.

Go ahead diet to be society thin.

Miranda smirked remembering that her co-worker Carol had commented she looked good, but a little too thin. How would a person who ate pizza for lunch know?

"Hey Pudgy.!" Miranda turned, but no one was there. Her brother's voice gently floated inside her brain. "Fatty Matty," teased at her ears.

SOCIETY THIN

At three, her older brother gave her the nickname of Pudgy, which her family thought cute. At six her mother put her on her first diet. She wasn't cute anymore.

Now days when family members called her Pudgy, Miranda rolled her eyes at them and whispered, more to herself, to please desist in calling her that, but the knot in her stomach remained. Her dad just laughed at her and pinched her cheeks like she was still six years old, instead of a twenty year old adult living on her own.

To tame her demons, Miranda also did step aerobics and zumba five nights a week. But no matter what she did, her body still retaliated against her and refused to give up the weight.

Today Miranda started her fast. She knew fasting would make her body as thin as she desired - imagined it should be, model thin.

During Miranda's second day of fasting, the dizziness and light headed came. She put her head down on her desk; she knew this feeling would pass after a short time.

After five minutes, Miranda started to feel better. All she wanted was a cool sip of water - trying to crush her desire for food.

She tried to sit up as Carol walked by her cubical eating a slice of pepperoni pizza.

"Miranda," Carol stopped, "Are you okay? You look a little flushed."

"I'm okay." Miranda tried to fake a grin, "I'm just need to close my eyes for a few minutes. Late night." The smell of the pizza was making her ill.

"You're not dieting again are you? I mean you look great."

"Thanks, Carol."

Miranda heard Carol exhale and continue. The smell lingered.

Miranda made a dash for the ladies room and heaved. Nothing came up and after a few minutes, the feeling passed. By drinking water, the sick feeling in her stomach, the dizziness, and the weakness disappeared. Soon she had no desire for food.

Miranda also achieved her greatest goal; she seemed to be getting thinner! However, when Miranda looked in the mirror her mind still saw fat. And the name Pudgy tore into her heart.

Miranda grew thinner. Her clothes sagged. Her scale registered 86 pounds.

Somehow Miranda still managed to function at work without eating. Her co-workers were whispering behind her back, *"She lost all that weight, but now......she must think she looks good, but how can she function looking like a corpse...I can't even look at her....she must have that disease, didn't her mother die a few years ago from..."* but no one confronted her.

Miranda heard, but chose their words - *"looks good."*

Miranda was down to a baggy size zero, but still "fatty Matty's" eyes stared back at her, followed her in mirrors, in shiny objects.

During her twelfth day of fast on her drive to work, the lines in the street crossed, cars whirled by her, her eyes blinked as her head swam. She tried to pull over when everything faded to black.

Intense pain echoed from Miranda's body awaking her.

Like a ghost, a white coated individual faded in.

"Miranda," the kind eyes focused on her, "I'm Doctor Carter, you're a very luck girl, only a few scratches and bruises."

All Miranda saw were tubes and needles. "I remember seeing blackness."

"Yes. Miranda," he paused, seeming to choose his words, "when was the last time you ate?"

Miranda turned to face the window, "I don't remember. I know I could probably stand to lose weight." Her voice grew weak.

Dr. Carter's voice echoed softly through Miranda's being, "Miranda, you have to start eating. Your body's showing signs of deterioration."

Miranda stared at the tubing, but made no comments. She nodded and tried to force her lips upward.

Dr. Carter had seen people like Miranda. He noted in her chart, "starvation for society sake."

Miranda tried eating the strawberry Jello, chicken broth, the hot tea, but felt sick with anything, except water. She flushed them down the toilet.

The nurses began bringing Miranda solid food and her requested chocolate. So she ate. Then retched. She saved the chocolates for her rewards.

After a week in the hospital, Miranda looked rested, but gained no weight.

The 5:00 A.M. weigh-ins were getting tiresome and weakness was setting in her bones. She craved aerobics and to run free. Dr. Carter noted she was eating and could no longer hold her. Her physical wounds were healed. He agreed to let her go home but chastened her about continuing to eat.

Miranda kept her promise and ate when people were present, but she quickly excused herself to the bathroom, puked, then applied chocolate chap stick. Then she jogged when she was free of concerned family members.

Miranda continued her routine for almost a month until fate stepped in and rendered her body useless at work. She tried to raise her head from her lunchtime snooze, but its heaviness restrained her. She whispered to the wind, "Carol?" She tried rising, then stumbled forward. A soft thump hit the carpet. "Carol?"

Miranda was admitted to the hospital in a coma.

She weighed 75 pounds. Her skin sagged, aging her twenty years.

Mercifully, death stepped in and stole her soul.

SOCIETY THIN

    go ahead —
        DIE to be society thin.

there's a new disease in this mixed up world.
grown women starving themselves to death
to be society thin
    or overdosing themselves with food
to prove they are normal, and then the ultimate
    betrayal when
their fingers find their throats and invite them to be
    society thin.

    go ahead,
        DIE to be thin.

set an example that your children will follow
and you'll raise a generation of body image haters.
twiggy still rages in our minds as the idea thin.
"i hate my body,
    i would DIE to be society thin."

there's an old disease in this all powerful america,
it started in the 70's when thin

was the absolute power and
self image hasn't been the same since-

we're all still DYING to be society thin.
    DIEt,
        DYING,
            dieT,
                DYING
to be thin...

METAMORPHOSIS

BY MAI VAUGHTER MANCHESTER

PAUL
"Ladies and Gentlemen, the vivacious, ever alluring Precocious!"

I love to strut my stuff. I've performed as many as three shows a night, seven nights a week. The audience gets caught up in my madness and I'm transported into their frenzy. I am Tina Turner. I arise to become Cher. I flatter MaDonna. Watch me change into any of the ten personalities I can portray. My voice range is as unbelievable as my assortment of wigs. The audience believe I am their clones come to life, but in reality I am a true impersonator and performer. Of course, Precocious isn't my real name, but then neither am I a real female.

My birth certificate reads Paul Justin Callery, Jr. I grew up lonely in Carter, Tennessee, in what would have appeared to many as a normal "male" childhood. I did the usual boy things while growing up - basketball, football, collected baseball cards, and the boy scouts. I sung in the church choir since words came out of my mouth. Yet I have one fascination, women and the way they wore their clothes. Most days I had sense enough to know what time it was and when to get out of my mother's room. But one day I was so caught up in getting the walk right. She caught me.

She found me dressed in her white with red strip four-inch high heels, her white Sunday-go-to-meeting-dress wrapped around me and held up by a big red belt, and the reddish lipstick she owned. Actually the lipstick was smeared on what was supposed to be my lips. I've always had trouble coloring inside the lines. Oh, and her brand new, $200.00 red hat laid under my right foot. It had just fallen off as I tried to turn too fast. I still remember the look upon her face. Her mouth flew open, but not an evil word escaped. Instead she inhaled a long sigh and turned away from me. But my mom was quick to compose herself. She just patted me on the head, removing her wig from my oversized head, which is the reason her hat wouldn't stay on, and murmured it was a phase I would grow out of. She often whispered upward towards God when she tried controlling her temper. She tried to turn her head, but I could see the tears lingering in the corner of her eyes. But just a single teardrop spilled down her cheek. She backhanded that tear off of her face real hard and then turned back around to face me. She went down on her knees. I thought she was getting ready to pray for my soul, but instead she pulled me into her arms real hard and hugged me.

Monday morning she took me to the meanest man I'd ever seen. His name was Sarge. And he was a kick butt karate instructor. I was the smallest student and the newest. I don't know what my mother told him, but on every occasion, I was his demonstration dummy. I spent so much class time vertical that I only learned one thing - how to do that karate yell, I was real good at that. And as if that wasn't torture enough, I had to join the boy scouts. If Mom had only known that Mr. Dimples, our leader, had more twist in his walk then I ever would attempt, she just might have left me at home alone. I was ten. I was grown.

At my fifth birthday party, my Dad went to the store to buy some more film for the camera. Every time I looked up, he'd say, "Smile." Before he left, he pulled me into his long strong arms and whispered into my ear, "to be happy, you have to be yourself." My mom was still crying when I woke up the next morning. I think I cried myself to sleep for at least a year. My Mom would kiss me good night and when the light went off, my tears started. No more bedtime stories Daddy style. He used to make his voice go real deep, then the next character would have this high female voice. I don't know what I did, but if I had it all over to do again, I'd be real good. Good enough so my Dad wouldn't leave us. We never saw him or the camera again.

When I started school, I was so shy. I would sit and stare at the older girls but not really them. I was paying close attention to their clothes, their jewelry, their makeup, their hairstyles, and most important, their mannerism. My classmates called me the queer boy, mostly because I never engaged in any conversations. I didn't want to talk to them, play with them, or be near them. I just wanted to observe the girls.

I lost my virginity at the young age of thirteen to Mira, a seventeen-year-old sophomore. Mira knew what the other kids thought, which made her come after me like a cat tiptoeing across a hot tin roof. She wanted to see if I really was "funny." She had already been though the senior class and was looking for more of a challenge. She changed my reputation with my classmates and my admiration for women became even stronger. We became friends, I didn't judge her and she didn't judge me. I became a good lover. In exchange for sex, Mira taught me how to apply makeup, how to walk lady style without all those extra twists in my hips, and other female tips, the rest I learned from my old baby-sitter - television when my mom finally let me stay at home by myself again.

Women are just beautiful, graceful, and I wanted to be one without really changing into one.

If you dream long enough, then reality sets in. I was 17 and a high school graduate. Mira brought my dream to reality. We only practiced for two weeks, but then she said I was ready. With a suitcase full of clothes, wigs, and make-up, Mira and I caught the first bus to Nashville, Tennessee, early Saturday morning. A new cabaret was hiring on Broadway. We stayed at some cheap motel two blocks down the street and try-outs were that Monday. I was nervous. The two blocks walk seemed like a hundred, but Mira stayed by my side. I entered dressed in a tight red mini-skirt, red halter-top, light make-up (I never could grow a beard), red fishnet stocking, four inch red pumps, and red glitter in my long curly blond hair. I saw the jealous looks in the other competitors' eyes as their stares stayed moments too long on me. I looked more like loud, bounteous, singing czar Bethe Midler then she did. I had her walk, her voice, her mannerism, and her aura. When I walked out on the stage I purposely stood a moment too long to let everyone honor me. I saw the owners' mouths drop. I knew I was in. I finished one stanza before I was stopped. I was hired on the spot. When asked my name, I said Precocious. Paul just didn't fit anymore. I was finally transformed. Mira kissed me on the cheek and I never saw her again. She said she had to follow her dream now. She headed for New York and the real Broadway.

I made enough money to keep me happy pretending to be someone else, besides, I looked better than most women; and men, they believed I was truly a woman. At the cabaret, men would come up behind me and grab my derriere. I just smiled, adjusted my boobs, and gave them my baritone voice. I don't know if they were hoping for a female or not. Some backed off with a surprised look on their face and others I had to signal for security to get them off of me.

You see, even though I loved to cross dress and imitate women, I preferred to sleep with women only. I loved women's softness - not the hard body of someone with all the parts I had. Their softness was the essence of my imitation.

I was nineteen and living fast and wild. The fact that I was a female impersonator was no secret; except to Mama. Several of my girlfriends had seen my performance. I was a beautiful woman, but I was manly enough to perform beyond any woman's wildest dream. Mira taught me well.

When I went out, unless I was meeting my girlfriend, I mostly went in drag. I got a kick out of all of the men flirting with me. And a free meal is a free meal, so I would accept their dinner invitations, but right before the goodnight kiss - I would say in my deepest male voice, "Have you ever done it with a man?" Then I'd look them deep into their eyes, and say, "That's right, you're about too." This usually sent them running, looking to make sure no one saw them.

JOHNNY

Johnny saw her in Hickory Hollow Mall as he was passing Frederick's of Hollywood. She was looking at lingerie. He entered the store and tried to sneak looks at her as she stood over silk black panties. Johnny had never seen anyone as beautiful, slender or as tall as she; legs for days. His pick up lines were dated but there was no way he was leaving this store without at least talking to her.

"Excuse me, but my sister is getting married and she's having a lingerie party. I've been elected by my brothers to buy her gift. I was wondering if you might help me?"

She turned and her soft voice whispered out, "I'm sorry, I don't work here."

Up close, her beauty seeped out, "I know that. I was hoping for a real woman's opinion. Please?"

"Okay, but everything comes with a price."

Her large brown eyes were drawing him in, "How's about dinner?"

"I was thinking more along the lines of you picking up my purchases. I'm Precocious."

"I'm Johnny. If you promise to have dinner with me."

"Monday night at 6:00. Buy her the white teddy with feathers. Every woman loves pretending to be pure on her wedding night."

"You speak from experience?"

"No, Johnny, but I know women." The words whispered out of Precocious' sensuous mouth. Precocious handed him her address. "Don't be late."

Johnny was almost out of the door when he heard her voice calling after him.

"I think you have forgotten something." Her voice trailed after him.

Johnny turned and Precocious stood at the register with two $200.00 white teddies in hand. He paid, carrying one white teddy with him. He walked so lightly, he thought he was floating. Johnny couldn't believe he had actually asked a beautiful woman for a date and she had accepted. This was going to be a new experience for him. His last real date had been junior year in high school. Johnny didn't date for free. He valued money and in his profession he had no choice which position his client preferred. Johnny dropped out of high school when he was introduced to fast money. He'd never had feeling for any of his clients, he just performed their delight, usually what their husband didn't give them. Sometimes, Johnny performed in front of their husbands and sometimes they joined in. He had gotten use to doing it in whatever oral capacity they desired. But to finally meet a woman that turned him on. Precocious definitely had possibilities. This Monday would have to be special. He needed big money to impress. So tomorrow and Sunday, the highest price would get their delight, so he could have his delight - Precocious. Johnny was sure she'd give in, all women did.

PRECOCIOUS

I was looking forward to my free dinner with Johnny and my metamorphosis into the female world. I could tell he was a big spender from the clothes and shoes he wore. Johnny was the best looking man I had ever met and for the fun of it, I considered letting him kiss me. Beautiful people should be allowed to come together in at least a kiss, but then I would have to tell Johnny the truth - I am a man. Who knows maybe this man would be the one to send me over the edge into the world of kinky sex.

JOHNNY

Johnny had rented a limo for his date with Precocious. He had also brought a dozen red and yellow roses. Yellow for friendship and red for danger ahead. First impressions must be good tonight. Johnny was planning on romancing Precocious from the minute she opened the door.

PRECOCIOUS

I wore my hair up and put on my red, almost to my panty line, dress. I knew my best assets were my long, slender, hairless legs. I also applied blood red lipstick to complete my outfit. I look good. I had learned from women the art of the tease in all of their movements. I consider myself the best actor around this little city. I could study a person for ten minutes and transform myself into that person. All my female dates found me charming, as they say, imitation was the only form of flattery.

DATE NIGHT

Johnny pulled up in a charcoal gray limousine. Johnny had on his new gray Armani suit, and he knew he was making a statement - rich, as he walked up to ring Precocious' doorbell.

Precocious opened the door and Johnny was looking at fire. She was so hot, Johnny was afraid to touch her. The roses worked prefect. Precocious smiled and kissed Johnny on the cheek.

Their conversation in the limo was electric, like they had known each other for years.

The restaurant, located at the top of Vanderbilt Plaza, was elegant and expensive. Johnny found himself flirting endlessly. Dinner lasted six hours, till midnight. Johnny could hold out no longer, but he wanted to let Precocious make the first move.

PRECOCIOUS

I turned to Johnny and purred softly, "Johnny, it's getting late and I have to work tomorrow, could you take me home?"

"Only if I can come in for a nightcap."

I had a hard time saying no, I was attracted to him. His breath on the back of my neck was driving me crazy. I lost myself and the words slipped out, "Most definitely."

JOHNNY

Johnny glanced away and smiled, he seemed to know he had scored.

PRECOCIOUS

The conversation in the limo was light. My heart was beating too fast to concentrate on words. I let Johnny hold my hand – mistake one.

Johnny quietly whispered something to the driver and helped me out of the limo. The limo disappeared around the corner as Johnny's beeper vibrated.

This date had turned out extra nice and I wondered how Johnny would take the news I had to divulge to him. If it wasn't for the fact I loved women and the kinky sex lifestyle just didn't exist for me, no matter how attractive the man - I might consider giving Johnny a try, but I couldn't see falling in bed with a man.

Johnny was lucky; I usually don't allow my male dates inside my door, no matter how good looking and entertaining they turned out to be – mistake two.

As I was pouring our drinks, Johnny put his arms around me. I turned and held my hand up. Johnny stopped and looked at me with this conquering quest in his eyes. I couldn't follow through, "I have something very important you need to know." The words were spilling out harshly before I could stop them, "Johnny, I'm not a woman."

Johnny's face turned shades of red and his breathing got rapid. Johnny then held up his hand and said, "No woman has ever given me that line before. Baby you've got to prove that."

This was a first, maybe my voice didn't go deep enough. I unwillingly took Johnny's hand and guided it towards my stockings. Even though the stockings, his touch was cold. Johnny felt my maleness. But he just smiled and said, "That's no problem, I enjoy going both ways and this will be a delightful first. You see, I've always wanted to do it with a drag queen. The best of both worlds."

He stood back and observed me. I felt like a pig at a slaughter house.

"Let's get started." He slightly grimaced.

I felt my heart stop; I had never faced this problem before. "Pardon me?" I said in my most masculine voice.

"I said I go both ways. So get undressed." His fingers touched my top button, then he pulled back and stared at me again. "I suppose the hair isn't real."

My mind would not think. Johnny's eagerness was growing. His eyes emitted the light of death. I was dead if I didn't do as his quiet shouts demanded. He out muscled me by several pounds.

JOHNNY

Johnny was growing tired of the game and he was madder than he'd ever been in his life. "I said get undressed, NOW!"

PAUL

I begged, but his anger extenuated from his face: his seemingly black eyes were growing in size, his thin lips parted, but words I refused to hear, the small hairs stood up on the back of his neck, and hatred poured from his pores. I had no choice; I closed my eyes and obeyed out of fear. My body still resisted in small ways, but Johnny found his way in.

After Johnny left, I was still in shock; I couldn't believe it had happened to me. None of my begging helped. I had been raped by a man and the evening was probably my fault.

JOHNNY

Johnny did not enjoy rough sex and felt he had almost raped Precocious. So he vowed never to see her/him again. Besides, he only screwed men for money, but he had felt betrayed and used. Johnny felt he should have been able to tell the difference; but Precocious seemed real. His mind drifted back to her long slender legs, round lips, and her small feet.

PRECOCIOUS/PAUL

The next day I called into work sick. This was the first time I had ever missed work. To get my mind off of what happened, I did my usual - I went shopping. I dressed in jeans, a sweater, tennis shoes and no make-up. And I pulled my long curly hair back into a ponytail. I looked in the mirror and a good-looking man stared back - suddenly dressing up in female clothing was no fun. I told no one what had happened - I was too embarrassed and I knew, in my heart, no one would believe a man had raped me.

I wished I could find Johnny, not to confront him, but to talk about what happened and to apologize for leading him on. I knew that Johnny's anger was in the deceit. Besides last night the reoccurring dreams - nightmares kept coming and I woke up in a cold wet bed. Today, I felt the need to pray. I made a promise never to date another man or woman without first revealing my true identity.

Before "it" happened, I had felt a brotherly love and I was attracted to Johnny. No man had ever stirred me before.

I contemplated quitting my job, but I realized it was the only thing I did well - impersonate women. Besides the unexplained actions of life must become a positive effect and one continues to survive.

I went back to work three nights later and when I performed, I found the usual peace - again I entered into the world that I had found as a child that I belonged in. The portrayal became the character or was I portraying? Tonight my metamorphosis took me to MaDonna - live and totally uncensored and exotic. I lived.

At the end of my 45 minutes performance, I looked over my audience and saw Johnny, sitting at a back table - smiling. His attire was too expensive for the cabaret.

I went back to my dressing room, took off my make-up, and changed into my new off stage generic outfit: jeans and sweater. I went to Johnny's table. His smile drew as I approached. My feelings were mixing inside my churning stomach.

"Precocious?"

"Yes, you may call me Paul. How did you know where to find me?" I tried to sound cold.

"I asked around. Precocious, turns out you're very well known in your profession. I admire a woman," He broke eye contact, "a man that's good in whatever his chosen profession is."

"Oh." I couldn't help the smile that came to my lips. My face betrayed me.

Johnny stared, "Except for the eyes, I wouldn't have known it was you. You're very good at what you do. You're very talented and beautiful on stage."

"Thanks, I've learned from the best. I guess I'm glad you stopped by, there is something, rather my dreams scream to be released. Unfortunately, but true, you taught me a lesson that I needed. I love women too much to put myself in that predicament again. And, I am sorry." I couldn't stand to look at him anymore. He is beautiful.

"No, I'm the one who needs to apologize. I'm sorry for what I did, but I was taken with you as a woman and I just felt deceived, plus I couldn't control my lust/anger." He looked away.

I tried looking back at him, my eyes adverted downward, "I'm sorry about the deceit. I've been doing it since I was thirteen and it just came naturally to be female on a date, but my dates usually only went so far. But if I was a woman, Johnny, I could have easily fallen for you."

Johnny blushed, "You know we're not that different. We both sell our bodies for profit. We're both performers."

"I don't know what you do for a living. Apparently you're doing very well. Your clothes, your shoes, give you away."

"I've been doing it, selling my body, since I was sixteen. It got me away from my crazy mother."

"Well, I just like dressing up and pretending to be a woman." I still hadn't figured out if he wanted anything else. "I have another set in twenty minutes, will you be staying?"

"No, I have a date. She's a regular. I'll be seeing you around, maybe we can shoot some hoops one day."

We both laughed at that statement. "I haven't done that since I was a kid. Have a good date." I started to rise.

"I will, she pays very well."

I stood towering over Johnny imaging the softness of his lips, "Thank you for stopping by to apologize. It means a lot to me."

"Well, there is another reason I stopped by." He stood, "I was thinking we could form a partnership. I have a lot of male and female customers who would love to date and sleep with you, in drags of course. It would be a fantasy come true for them, the best of both worlds. I promise, you could make thousands of dollars a night." His hand rose towards my face, but the plea in my eyes must have stopped him.

My heart jumped, I found myself smiling, "No thanks, I'm not ready to go that far." My voice dropped, "I prefer women. I've got to go, you know make-up and all."

"Good-bye." His voice trailed after me.

I went to my dressing room to begin putting on my make-up, but I felt Johnny's eyes following the illusion he desired. I wondered why Johnny would go to the trouble of looking me up for such an odd arrangement. At least now maybe the nightmares would stop. It turned into a strange conversation - two minutes till show time - I was dressed and pumped up. Tina Turner, your legs were cloned from mine. I escaped into my world.

JOHNNY

Johnny stayed to see Precocious next performance, postponing his weekly date with 60-year-old Debbie. He would miss the $3,000 compensation, but the Grand Marnier warmed his soul. Precocious was alluring. Those long exotic legs, Johnny felt himself grow hard. Precocious stared unadulterated at him and her voice entered his heart. He left for home with Precocious bellowing out, "What's Love Got To Do With It?" He took one look back; they would make a charismatic couple. The slight chill in the air felt good upon his cheeks, he thought of the money they could make. He knew he would arrange his schedule to return to the alluring Precocious. He knew she would succumb, women always did.

Johnny lives in a $1,000,000 condo on the west side. He stands 6'6", possesses the face of Adonis and a slender muscular body that men and women show their desire for. Since the age of sixteen, he has enjoyed the sport of selling his body.

He heaved his frame into his customized black Mercedes and drove from lower Broadway humming, "What's Love Got to Do With it?" contemplating his next prohibited visit with Precocious.

FRIDAY'S RITUAL

BY MAI VAUGHTER MANCHESTER

Jason half rose, smiled, and waved to Mitzi from a booth in the bar section of O'Charlies'.

"I'm sorry I'm late. Have you been waiting long?"

"Not really. I hope this is okay." Jason's right hand trembled as he took his pack of Kools out of his jacket pocket and tapped it on the table.

"Yeah. It's fine." Mitzi slid into the booth and glanced at the ashtray, which held two half burned cigarettes. "I got your voice mail. What was so important that we change our usually Friday dinner to tonight?"

Jason steadied his hand and lit his Kool. He inhaled long and slow, whirling smoke rings as he exhaled. "Chris is joining us." He slowly enunciated.

"Chris? Oh. It's been two weeks since, you know. My calls weren't even returned." Mitzi unconsciously whirled the engagement ring on her finger. "I suppose I should give the ring back."

A waitress appeared placing an order of Buffalo wings, ice water with lemon, and two Miller Lites in front of them. Mitzi stared at the meat. She had been a vegetarian for six months, and the smell of the cigarettes mixed with the odor of beer and chicken was beginning to make her nauseated.

Mitzi half smiled at the waitress, "Could I have a coffee?"

"Sure, do you want that with cream and sugar?"

"No." Mitzi shook her head. The waitress' heels clicked on the tile floor and vibrated through Mitzi's head.

Jason stared at the hockey game on the television over the bar. He crushed his half burned cigarette out.

"So, why is Chris coming?" Mitzi asked sounding disinterested.

"Just to talk. You know, Chris is moving to San Francisco next month."

The catch in Mitzi's voice was too loud. "Oh. I heard." Mitzi's eyes lowered.

"And," Jason continued slowly waiting to make eye contact with Mitzi, "I've given my two weeks' notice."

Mitzi stared at Jason, mouth open but no sounds escaping. She cleared her throat.

Jason slowly nodded.

The waitress returned with Mitzi's coffee. "Are you ready to order?"

"No, I'll just have coffee."

"Nothing else for now." Jason refocused on the game.

Mitzi put ice cubes in her coffee and quickly gulped it down. She stood up, "I'm sorry, Jason, I've got to get home. I forgot Terrye is supposed to be coming over." Her words tripped over each other.

"I'll see you tomorrow." Jason lit another cigarette.

"Yeah." Mitzi turned and saw the smiling blond headed Chris that she still loved coming in their direction. Mitzi turned in the other direction and headed for the bathroom.

A LIFE FOR A LIFE

Pendal Gail Deliverance had waited most of her life for this moment. From the time she was a little girl, she had been lead to believe by her mother that this was what made life worth it - it made her a woman. And the fact that she was forty years old and experiencing life's moment for the first time did not make the pain less or the work enjoyable. Pendal had a hard time concentrating on the moment; she truly wanted to be unconscious.

"Push Pendal!" A shout from a faint distant voice.

With her last exhalation, she obeyed. She felt as if she was giving birth to a ball of fire, but finally pain and the pressure became one and relief arrived.

The joy of motherhood arrived in the sound of a high-pitched, emotion-filled, first cry of ecstasy, confusion, and first breath of life on his own. Entered Calvin Munford Deliverance.

Pendal was quietly sobbing, not from joy, but the fact that her entrance into motherhood was finally over.

The nurse placed Calvin into her arms and Pendal looked at Calvin, who had so far caused her sixteen hours of pain. She searched for the instant euphoria. She found none; however, she knew joy would come. After all, this was her mission in life; being a mother was what made her a woman.

Calvin cried, wet, and ate. Pendal cried and ate.

Pendal's Aunt Helen, mother of seven, assured her that everything was fine and that all would eventually fall into place.

Pendal wept; Calvin wailed.

Pendal's venture into motherhood could be crowned an accident. During her pregnancy, Pendal could not bring herself to tell Calvin's father, Yong Bellephant. She unconsciously hoped that silence would make her condition disappear.

For the first five months, Pendal convinced herself that she was going through the change in life. However, when all her weight started to center below her waist and in her hips, she finally went for a pregnancy test. And the "rabbit died", as her love affair with Yong had "died" months earlier.

So Pendal had four months to convince herself that her mission in life was finally upon her.

Enter Calvin Munford Deliverance.

Aunt Helen, who loved babies, was at Pendal's door before sunrise. Pendal did not mind; she and Calvin had spent the night sobbing and devouring massive quantities of food. Within six weeks time, Pendal put on twelve pounds, the weight she lost giving birth.

Pendal slowly realized that motherhood was not her mission in life. Where was the exhilaration? Where was the love? Where was her life?

Pendal returned to work at Flintstone Realty, happily dropping Calvin off at Aunt Helen's doorstep. She was now fifteen pounds heavier. Co-workers innocently asked when she was going to deliver. Pendal resounded, "Never."

For the past six weeks, Pendal's discussions had been with the less than six-week-old Calvin, and her sixty-year-old aunt - conversations did not come easy.

Within the past six months, Pendal had sold one house. This would not get her back in the million-dollar circle sales club - where her sales had been before Calvin penetrated her world. First she blamed her pregnancy for the loss in sales, then she blamed Calvin, now her excess weight.

Calvin was growing on her. After all, he was as beautiful as his father. She just didn't understand why other women felt they had to have a miniature human person pulling every ounce of mental and physical energy from them. Her mother must have been completely crazy when she informed her of her mission in life. She now not only hated her mission in life, she had also lost her enthusiasm for sales. Tears found her again.

Pendal spent her days attempting to sell houses and her nights walking the floor with Calvin. Pendal cried as Calvin cried. She did not know what it was to sleep in her own bed, to have a social life, to smell someone that did not smell like a baby, or to be held by two strong powerful arms. But come to think of it, that was how she got Calvin; wanting to be in his Herculean arms.

When Pendal was little, she had every doll on the market. Being an only child, her parents showed love the best they could, by showering her with gifts. Pendal spent most of her younger years with one baby-sitter or another. Mother never allowed her to stay with Aunt Helen; too many kids, too many germs. It seemed Mother was always planning some trip or some party to take Father away from her. She vowed then that her child would have her undying love.

But now she realized why Mother chose to stay away so much. When Pendal made her vow she did not realize she would be forty starting off motherhood, or that she would be alone.

Walking the floors at night, Pendal spent time thinking about how old she would be when Calvin was sixteen, she would be 56 - time for a cane and a rocking chair. Pendal realized that if Calvin grew up to be like Yong, he would have the physique of a body builder, the looks of a model, and the brain with the thinking capacity the size of a pea. Looks had definitely been deceiving in Yong's case.

Pendal inhaled and thought she smelled the essence of "Beware" - Yong's favorite cologne. Rocking Calvin to sleep, she closed her eyes and traveled back to the beginning of her pure lust.

Pendal stared at the man she saw in front of her.

Pendal was supposed to be shopping for a Mother's Day present - not that her mother was deserving, but a simple "thank you" from her mother was better than hearing what an unappreciative daughter she was. Right now she hoped to pick up something besides perfume.

Pendal eased closer to the perfume counter, closer behind the blond, dreadlocked, ponytail-wearing, tanned Adonis. He must be at least 6'5", with the physique of a tri-athlete, and a derriere so tight she could bounce quarters off it. Oh, and check out his thighs - nothing but muscle. How could one human being possess so many perfect features?

Pendal contemplated how to flirt. She recalled Gail, from <u>If This Be the Beginning,</u> her favorite soap opera, and nervously presumed her persona.

"That's a great perfume, gift for your wife?" Pendal did not realize she had spoken.

Yong slowly turned to face her.

Pendal face glowed with anticipation.

After what felt like hours under his indifferent gaze, she heard what she wanted.

"No."

Pendal felt like a child anxiously anticipating consuming her mom's prized apple pie.

"Oh, girlfriend?" *Her heart accelerated.*

Still under his magical piercing stare, Pendal inhaled and forgot to breath. Her only thoughts were that this god was taken. Why else would he take so long in delivering a simple no? She felt her face turning all shades of bright red under her auburn skin.

"No, it's not."

Panting, Pendal uttered, "Well, could I interest you in dinner tonight?" *She was not accustomed to picking up men. When she was young, girls would not dream of calling a boy on the telephone for fear of being thought loose, but this was 2002.*

Yong looked Pendal straight in her mystifying brown eyes; she felt herself melting under his undressing gaze. She was glad she still maintained her size eight figure and had the legs of Tina Turner; or so she imagined when she daydreamed in front of her mirror. Pendal found herself holding her breath waiting for Yong's long awaited answer.

"I'd love to."

Pendal wondered if she was supposed to pay. "I'm Pendal." *She held out her hand.*

"Pendal?"

"Yes, and you're?"

"Yong." *Soft lips greeted Pendal's hand.*

"Yong?" *A whisper escaped Pendal.*

"Yeah." *He kissed her fingertips and then released her hand. A smile escaped the sides of his lips.*

"Well, Yong, where might I meet you?" *Pendal was not sure if she was supposed to pick him up.*

"How's about Arthur's, about 7:00?"

"That's a great restaurant. See you tonight." Pendal smiled then turned on shaky legs. She could still feel Yong undressing her with his piercing gray eyes. This was the first time she had ever asked a man for a date - a perfect stranger.

Pendal saw Yong for three months - three months of sexual, sensual lust.

The more Pendal thought about it, she wondered if Yong should be told he had a son. Yong had been great for her mental image, a 40 year old woman dating a 25 year old "boy". He had also been great for her libido, the best lover she ever had - but on the conversation end he lacked the intelligence to go beyond five minutes before he had his clothes off. Pendal only imagined what Yong did for a living; he was always available on a minute's notice.

Calvin was finally asleep. Pendal put him down and wondered about the amazement of giving life. She had given life to Calvin, but she questioned what her life would have been like without her father. She decided to track down Yong. They could not be lovers again, however, he might desire to know his son.

The next day, Pendal, remembering her junior detective training, began her search for Yong. She called the last number she had for him. John, his roommate, said he had moved out last month. She pretended to be Yong's cousin from out of town, just passing through and wanting to say "Hi!" The deceit worked. John told her that Yong had moved in with Susie Mahap on the east side of town. Pendal thought that Yong was probably using his good looks to get a free ride again. She wondered how Yong would react to hearing he was a father, or if he would even believe that Calvin was his.

Pendal unconsciously dressed in her sexiest too-tight red dress and on a steamy July morning, Pendal took three-month-old Calvin to introduce him to his father.

At 8:00 A.M. she waited patiently for the woman to exit the house for work. Yong probably never worked a day in his life. Pendal's thoughts were roaming from male stripper to male escort, when the door opened. Just as she thought, his mistress seemed to be in her late thirties, chubby, hair that blew in the wind, but she didn't have Tina Turner's legs. Pendal had to smile at the thought that she was more beautiful, but her smile quickly faded as she realized that Yong must really be a Casanova.

Walking slowly to the door, clutching Calvin, Pendal inhaled and knocked. Exhaling, she found her breathing was rapid as she waited for Yong to answer the door. The morning was already hot and sticky. Pendal wiped her brow with Calvin's spit-up cloth. Calvin was actually smiling at her as he seemed to coo "thank you mommy," but suddenly her red dress seemed too tight and too hot. Someone was finally opening the door. Pendal smiled when she saw Yong staring confusedly at her.

"Pendal?"

"Hi, Yong."

Yong's face went from confusing to disbelief. "What are you doing here? How did you find me?"

"I want you to meet someone. This is our son, Calvin."

Yong's answer was hysterical laughter, but seeing her maintain a straight face, his laughter ceased.

"Yong, I'm not kidding. This is your son, Calvin."

"How? No, don't answer that." Yong kept looking over her shoulder. "Why don't I meet you at Arthur's in thirty minutes. I can't talk here."

Before Pendal could answer, she found the door slamming in her face. Pendal drove to Arthur's, took a table in the corner, ordered a glass of orange juice, settled Calvin with his bottle, and commenced to wait.

An hour passed before Yong showed up.

Pendal saw Yong enter the restaurant. He had more muscles than she remembered, but he still looked the same - caramel ice-cream that she could devour. Pendal knew she was doing this for her son; she had to keep her lust in check. "Don't even think about smiling, this is for Calvin, not your libido." She found herself consciously thinking.

"I didn't think you were coming."

"Neither did I. Pendal, you're telling the truth? This is my son?"

"Yes!"

"How old is he?"

"Calvin is three months old."

Yong stared at Calvin. "He does look a little like me. He has my hair, my eyes," turning his focus back to Pendal, "What do you want from me?"

"I want Calvin to know his father."

"What else? You of all people should know I don't have money. And I'm not exactly the fatherly type." Yong's voice was beginning to attract attention.

"I don't want your money. I just want to know if you want to be a father to <u>your</u> son?" Pendal whispered.

"I don't know if I can. I mean, Pendal, you show up with this three month old baby and tell me I'm a father and all of a sudden I'm suppose to become a father. I mean you must admit you didn't give me any warning. Why did you wait till now to tell me when life is finally beginning to look up for me. Why didn't you tell me when you were pregnant?"

"Yong, it's a long story," Pendal felt slightly disgusted, "but I'm telling you now that you are Calvin's father." Not knowing what else to do, Pendal rose. "You know where to reach me when you decide you want to be Calvin's father. Don't wait too long."

Pendal, holding back her tears, gathered Calvin up and walked out - not knowing if she would ever see Yong again. She stopped and took a glance back, Yong only sat gazing into empty space. She thought she could sense he wanted to reach out, but was afraid of their future. Pendal knew this Don Juan could only take care of himself. She just prayed she would never fall victim to another Yong Bellephant.

Pendal sat in her car wiping tears for five minutes. She could see Yong still sitting in the restaurant staring into space. Within their brief encounter, she had learned to read the expressions on his angelic face. Pendal thought she saw Yong dab a napkin to the corner of his eyes, or was she only hoping that Yong would return to her.

Suddenly, while watching Calvin smiling and cooing at her, and kicking his fat little legs, Pendal realized she had a fulfilling life ahead of her. She watched Yong exit the restaurant and turn toward his woman on the east side. Pendal knew that Yong was forever lost to her and her precious child would only have her to give him the love of a parent. Pendal had traded her life for a life existing with Calvin - her undeniable, desirable mission in life.

THE BARN

I had bought the six-acre milking farm with the intentions of tearing down the house, barn, and silo, but I wasn't prepared for what greeted me inside the badly painted black dilapidated barn. This made for an interesting dilemma. The house held no treasures and had long been condemned, and the silo was the feeding nest for neighborhood cats and rats. The greedy side of me only thought of the money to be made from breaking the land into 12 half-acre tracts and building million dollar homes, but to honor my father, who had been a tenant farmer in his childhood, I had to take a look at the inside of the barn.

On the loft door was a freshly painted American flag and "We shall not be moved". I thought a patriotic passer-by had probably painted it; after all, the property had been for sale "as is" for six years.

The wind cried out and the loft stood partially opened, and I saw the beginning of what seemed like a living memorial to an unfriendly war. My father had died in that unpopular war. Some did come home but no one celebrated, no one wanted to care, and there were no war heroes in the eyes of America. But inside this barn, someone cared. I scaled the rickety stairs, careful to miss the cracks and holes, to get a visual look. I shrieked as a rat tiptoed across my foot. As long as it wasn't a spider or snake, I told myself, I was okay. Did spider's webs mean spiders lurked nearby? Maybe they were afraid of the light and wouldn't come out. I'm halfway there, but my hands held steady to the fractured railing. I shined the light and a black object with yellow eyes peeked back. I focused and was greeted by a friendly "meow". I breathed a little easier and ascended to the hayloft. Sunlight beamed through the decaying slotted planks. The cat rubbed against my brown leather trousers taking my fear away.

I took a closer look at the walls. Some paintings were faded with time, but some seemed still wet with oil. Fifteen feet wide and honoring the Vietnam War from 1970 - 1972, with an American flag flying held up by an AK-47 rifle; B-52 planes dropping bombs on faceless images; distorted faces of American college students protesting, Kent State; a young man with smiling eyes dressed in military uniform making a peace sign; and then a tombstone with angles guarding the night. I could only make out 1952 -1972 and "I love you son". All the other words were lost with time. But my thoughts passed over the memories my mother relived of my father who had died in Vietnam in '72, one year after my birth.

I reached down and rubbed Samson's long black hair. Amazing how we name things we think we own. Samson purred and I could feel his vibration through my palm. I was compelled to touch the painting. Parts of it gave the illusion of being wet as if someone tried to touch-up the paint. The artist's talents had definitely improved over time. I traced the outline of the tombstone and death touched my heart.

I gathered Samson in my arms and left someone's memories behind. Tomorrow they shall bulldoze the barn.

REMEMBRANCE

It is old. So old no one knows it origins. There are stories, of course; there are always stories. But the story I'm going to tell you is true. I know it's true because it happened to me.

In the summer of 1985, I wander down a worn path that seemed to lead to nowhere. The hedges are thick and surrounded most of the trail, but the grassless dirt is what makes it a path. I have not seen the star pointed leaves with red berries of the hedges except in stories that my Great-Grandmother told in my youth. Those tales were always preceded by the warning – *"It will happen to you."*

The facts that I have run out of gas, know I am several miles from my mapped destination, and that there are no other signs of human life are what induce me to continue down this worn-out route.

I slap at what I think is a twig playing with my ear, but it's the whispers of my late Great-Grandmother Geneva, *"The third sin, Adam."*

A thump, a murmur, I hide my face, shield my ears, but the words keep repeating themselves.

"The third sin!" The voice inside my head grows louder.

I digress with my dreams taking me back twenty years.

"*The first sin, Grandmother, is,*" from the time I was five years old, my twin sister Ellen and I lived with our mother's grandmother and daily she taught us the ten sins of our life as she quoted them from her faded red journal. I always got them right; whereas, Ellen sadly could not remember past the first two and those she reversed.

"*It's important that you remember them exactly, Adam.*" She would smile, as she rubbed my brow and handed me chocolate kisses.

"*I will Grandmother.*" I was happy and life was simple in those days.

I slip and grab for air, but something keeps me on track. With arms as my guards, I fight my way through the dense bush. The only scratches I receive are to my right forehead. I lick my index finger and seal the blood.

A cottage appears before me. The one I have held in my dreams for over twenty years. My heart race. I know this dwelling touches my third sin.

The first sin is birth. The second sin is life. The third sin is... my mind recoils.

I must concentrate on the moment. I am not a child and those were unrealistic thinking of an old woman that insanity welcomed five years before her death.

Why then when I am experiencing life's joys do these transgressions appear so vividly? My first love's death? My son's death? Am I the originator of sin that compels all sins? Why were Great-Grandmother's stories of those ten sins haunting me and not Ellen? Ellen married and gave birth to my beautiful niece, Eve. Death has not touched Ellen.

Smoke swirls from the crumbling red chimney of the cottage. Metal bars accent the painted black windows. No light reflects outward. The dark clay brick reminds me of chocolate.

I stand poised to knock. *"Remember, Adam, the third sin."* taunts my ears.

"Grandmother, the third sin is..."

"Can I help you?" The words come rapidly at me and take my breath away. I stand before an elf-like woman with eyes the color of sunrise, hair like cotton candy, and deep dredged lines accenting sadness upon her face. Arms folded, she does not move. Yet in her is something familiar.

She stares up at me. "You shouldn't have come," Her voice softens, "Adam."

"How do you know my name?" I stammer. I try to control the quickness of my breath.

Her mouth squeezes together in old woman form unwilling to let secrets out. Her wrinkles highlight the downward curve carved into her face. She steps backwards and motions me in. Familiarity compels me to enter.

Two Tiffany lamps accent the smoked glass end tables. Next to the fireplace are two red Queen Ann chairs. Antiques fill every corner; except for a black faded sofa that reminds me of Great-Grandmother's which sits in the center of the cluttered room. Mirrors, in the pattern of crosses, adorn all four walls. I try to find her reflection, but her voice tickles my ears.

"Stories you have heard," she monotonously recites, her unblinking eyes gazing upward, "of the ten sins of your life. Told to you by Geneva, your earthly great-grandmother. One is birth."

My chest heaves as if someone has punched me. I grab the end of the couch to strengthen my legs.

"The first you abolished when you brought forth your child, Peter, who erased your sin of birth with his life. Two is life."

My breath accelerates and I fight the tears in remembrance of Peter.

"Delores," she continues, "your first love, renewed yours when her life was taken upon your child's birth. Three is..."

"Stop it! Stop it!" I ran to the door and grab for the knob that no longer exists. I am a prisoner. Her words assault me and hold me captive. I cannot look at her.

"You know you shouldn't have come." Her words are soft but harsh, "You should have obeyed the warnings, they were all for you. I am the third sin. Three is love." She shuffles as she moves closer, "I am your mother. I loved you enough to give you up. But now..." Her voice trails off and her silence causes me to turn.

Her eyes have grown cloudy with tears. She seems even smaller. The lines on her face have carved themselves deeper.

"Our sins are old." So softly her voice expels that I have to listen harder. "No one knows how or when yours originated. You know the stories Adam and they are happening to you." She looks up. Her eyes hold pain. "Adam, beware the seven sins you have left. You must warn Eve." Her eyebrows frown, "You shouldn't have come."

I reach for her.

"No." She chatters, folding her hands in prayer fashion up to her lips. She closes her eyes and softly chants. "Our sins are old. Four is..."

The door burst open and emits a burning bright hot light into the room. I fall down to my knees, close my eyes, and cradle my body to protect myself. When all is quiet, I blink my eyes open and unfold. I search the darkness for the figure that calls itself my mother. I find only a golden black tipped feather where she once stood.

A bitter wind enters my soul. I shiver. The door creaks slowly open and a cold gush rushes pass me. I pick up the feather and leave with the given wisdom to battle our sins.

"Your fourth transgression, Adam? You must remember. Survive and warn Eve." My mother's message remains within me.

"Yes." I nod and clutch the feather.

POPSICLE STICKS TO MY TONGUE

When I was a little girl, my mom would make the best popsicles. Mom would mix strawberry kool-aid, my favorite, and pour the mixture into Mickey Mouse popsicle trays. After supper, I would have my very own dessert while my mom and dad would have to eat cake. Misty, my dog, and I would run outside to play before the sun disappeared into darkness. Within a few minutes my strawberry pop was gone and Misty and I would play stick the popsicle stick on my tongue. Misty job was to jump high enough to grab the stick while chasing me. Before I knew it, darkness had almost enveloped us and Misty had chased me all over our yard and salty sweat would trickle down the bridge of my nose. Misty had the advantage because I would always sneak my mom's lug-soled shoes to run and play in.

That was twenty years ago. When I want to be enveloped in those memories, I'd go buy popsicles and watch strawberry red melt on my deck as the sun slowly disappears behind the horizon. I'd stick the popsicle stick on my tongue as Misty sits starring at me out of her one good eye. I even let the sweat trickle down the bridge of my nose and stick my tongue up to taste the memories. I watch darkness greet the night as Misty sits content with her paw resting on my mom's lug-soled shoes.

PURPLE PASSION

Sandy glanced over her shoulder into her dresser mirror and squinted. *No surprises*, she thought. Her reoccurring dream had left her drained. She relaxed on her back.

Wonder what death feels like? She mumbled. Flowers died and regenerated themselves each year. Her purple passion plant was now in its dormant stage. It produced two seedlings a year; one she carefully cultivated and replanted. The other she consumed. Natasha, as she affectionately named her plant, had been her grandmother's, passed down for generations to the females in the Bronzewith family. Sandy didn't believe the myth about Natasha, yet her dreams left her wondering.

Natasha was not planted in soil, but embedded within a smooth black rock. The legend was that Natasha was over four hundred years old and her seeds contained powers that produced a euphoric state. Sandy's grandmother had given the rock to her three years ago on Christmas Eve. "You are the next chosen one," her grandmother had said upon lovingly leaving the gift with her.

The next morning Sandy marveled at the two purple flowers that had grown and bloomed overnight. In the center of each bloom was a seed. Sandy followed her grandmother's instructions. She placed one seed back under the rock and the other she grounded up, placed in hot water, and consume as if it was tea. *Tasteless*, she thought. The first time she drank because of her promise to her grandmother to follow the tradition; her grandmother died two days later. The following years, she drank because her body craved it.

Last night had been the second dream. The vision always came two days after her fix and on the date of her grandmother's death.

The effects of the purple passion left Sandy exhausted and dazed for weeks. Sandy grabbed for her glasses and upon arising felt the urge to brush her teeth. She noticed the red markings around her neck. They appeared to be finger marks, but that was not possible. She also noticed the stains of red splattered over her right cheek. She inhaled loudly. Her blond hair held specks of black. She tried to refocus upon her dream. Nothing. She dragged a hot wet washcloth across her face and hair in hopes of erasing the phantoms of last night.

Sandy's door burst open and a petite redhead appeared. "Hey Sandy!"

"Bridget, I've told you and told you, don't just burst into my room. Learn to knock! Okay?"

Bridget rolled her eyes, "Next time I won't even bother coming." Bridget tossed Sandy's Sunday paper on the bed, turned her small frame, and started to exit.

"Wait. What's so important?" Sandy eyed her roommate.

Bridget turned to face Sandy. "You have a delivery." Bridget's mouth could hardly hold her teeth.

"What kind of delivery?"

Bridget said nothing more. She motioned Sandy into the living room.

Sandy dropped her washcloth in the sink and followed. The living room contained one-dozen black roses, one-dozen red roses, and two-dozen purple pansies.

"Who died?" Sandy turned to her roommate.

"I guess you. Now, come on read the card?" She handed Sandy a small purple envelope addressed to Sandra.

"Sandra, midnight will never be forgotten. I'll call you tomorrow. Tony"

"Well, what does it say or should I ask what did you do to deserve all these flowers? You know, I've never really seen black roses before. I know reds for love, but black? Death? You better be careful, you never know about people you meet. Come on Sandy, what does the card say? You're got to tell me. Is it from someone you know? Did you meet him last night?"

Sandy finally glanced in Bridget's direction, "Last night? I've got a headache." She reentered her room and locked the door. Her breathing was labored. Heart racing, she cupped her hands on her chest to calm herself. She remembered nothing. She thought she'd slept the night away. Sandy sat on the edge of her bed, closed her eyes, and willed herself to think. *Why midnight?*

Bridget's Kid Rock's "Devil Without a Cause" blared from the living room, clouding Sandy's thought process.

Sandy concentrated and images of her beautiful Natasha appeared. She smiled. Sandy had developed a ritual for Christmas day: candlelight, "The Phantom of the Opera" playing in the background, while wearing her red sheer gown. She then drank the tasteless addictive liquor. Images of a masked man appeared as she tried to replay the night. Sweat oozed from her palms. Her chest hurt.

The phone rang bringing her to the present.

"Hello." A quiet voice from within Sandra screamed out.

Sandy heard familiar music playing in the background.

"Hello? Hello!"

"Sandra, have you read the paper? Front page." A raspy male voice asked. "In dreams you will come to me and speak my name. Thank you again my life-giving angel."

Before she could answer the music stopped and Tony's faint familiar voice was gone. Sandy shivered and for a moment she thought her rock glowed.

She glanced at the paper at the foot of her bed. Leaning forward, she tried to read the front headlines. "Masque" caught her eye. She reached for the newspaper. "Masquerade Killer Strikes Again. It was around a year ago last Christmas when the Masquerade Killer last murdered. The body of another young male prostitute was found this morning. Like the others, he was only wearing a painted on red mask and specks of black dye in his hair that spelled out Natasha. The victim had finger markings on his neck and time of death was placed around midnight."

Sandy removed her glasses and wept. Her body continued to crave for Natasha. Dream filled memories haunted her. "Natasha."

IF TOMORROW

Clarence cautiously climbed the rail overlooking the Cumberland River keeping his eyes focused on his hands. He felt like a chimpanzee but he hadn't gathered the courage to fall forward. Perched up high, Clarence felt the intensity of his heart beating. His mind wanted to leap, but his hands had an iron grip.

"Who are you!?" She appeared instantly. Her piercing green eyes demanded attention.

Startled, Clarence almost lost his hold. Before he could answer, she was tugging on him. He wasn't sure if she was pushing him off or pulling him down.

"Get out of my space!" Her soprano voice sung out.

Clarence only stared at the imp of a girl and gripped tighter.

"I said, get out of my space!" She yanked harder and Clarence lost his footing. He tumbled downward and blissfully hit concrete. Pain issued from his forehead. He wiped the wetness from his brow and discovered a thin layer of blood, but he was alive. Blinking the blood out of his eye, he again stared into the hardened eyes of a young barefoot girl wearing an oversized green jumper.

"You almost killed me." Clarence's words sounded ironic to himself.

"Me, you're the one playing Superman. Weren't you going to fly off the bridge? I only made you go in a livable direction." She taunted him.

"I wasn't going to jump. I was only looking at the power of the river." Before Clarence could speak another lie, she was off and running.

"Hey, who are you?!" Clarence's voice echoed in the darkness.

The slenderized figure turned, tipped her yellow cap, revealing long red curls, and laughingly whispered, "The wind."

In the blink of Clarence's eyes, she was gone. Confused that his only injury was the cut over his eye, Clarence gazed past the street light, into the beauty of the heavens. Every star smiled down on him, as the moon seemed to laugh with a clownish grin. A gush of wind pushed him toward home and a brighter tomorrow.

REVELATION

Her worn down three inch heels pointed east and west as Clara Louise swaggered down the street. She hated that familiar flesh-slapping-flesh sound as her thighs rubbed to create fiction. As she breathed, she panted, creating sounds of a small whistle rising, but this was just the normal sounds of her intake of oxygen. Every step was strained as she moved her body, pulling her massive behind along. Onward she labored to reach her destination. She had only walked one block, yet her clothes were wet as sweat rolled off her forehead.

It was a beautiful 100-degree day in August.

Clara Louise Longhorn stood only five feet five, and had been told by Dr. Smithing that if she did not lose weight she would be dead by the time she was thirty. But in a hidden corner of her mind, her father's voice kept haunting her, "You know what a bone feels like, don't you Clara Louise? That's what a man doesn't want to feel. He wants a woman with warmness he can wrap his arms around." She figured in two more years, she'd be dead even if Daddy was right. Clara continued on her journey with every labored step. Passer-byes stared. Clara looked the other way after giving them her don't mess with me look. She refused to let strangers dictate her life; everyone couldn't have a fashion model's physical structure.

Clara was attempting harder to prove Daddy right in the last few months. She smiled and flirted her eyelashes at every seemingly available man. And her labors had finally paid off; last night at the Food Lion she had finally met someone: Tyrone. That man was gorgeous and he had actually carried on a conversation with her; even though his attention seemed more directed at her 44DDDs.

Clara stopped. If she could rest for ten minutes she could probably walk faster and get to her destination on time. Sitting, she felt like she had dived into the softness of her bed instead of a concrete bus stop. Clara's right leg started involuntarily jumping. Her nerves were attacking her. Denny's was just one more block. She was surprised that Tyrone had actually called the next morning and asked her out. Her first date in over two years. Denny's sounded like a great place to meet and she had agreed. Of course, Cleopatra was horrified that she had accepted a date to meet a stranger and at Denny's! What would her skinny roommate know about wanting a man to like her? She dated a different man every weekend. Cleo's words still rang in her head.

"Clara, you can't be serious? You're not going to go out with a guy after talking to him for five minutes," Cleo had her left hand on her hips, eyes oversized, right finger wagging in Clara's face, and her head was shuffling side to side, "and let me get this right, you met him at a grocery store and you're going to DENNY'S?"

"I'm not your child." Clara spat back at her.

"Okay, I'm sorry." Cleo heaved a deep breath, "Why don't we do this? Meet him here, get to know him a little bit first, and let me get a good look at him. You know, he's less likely to pull anything if he knows someone could identify him. You know I'm only looking out for your best interest, roomy."

Clara just left her standing there. Cleo must think she was dumb. She was not about to introduce Tyrone to her 38-24-38, smooth almond skin, scandalous clothes wearing roommate. And not to mention her roommate's derriere caused most men to sneak a second look. She needed the love this time.

Refreshed, Clara continued the one block to meet her, hopefully, new boyfriend. Inches away from the door her hand froze. *What would she say?* Negative thoughts infiltrated her mind. *Clara you know you're fat. He probably won't even show up. What were you really thinking? Boyfriend?*

"Clara?"

Clara's heart jumped into her throat as she stood frozen. She could not turn around.

"Clara Longhorn? Don't tell me you've forgotten me? Turn around and let me get a look at you. You've grown into a beautiful woman."

Clara turned to face the friendly smile of her high school Algebra teacher. "Mr. Gunner, how are you?"

"You may call me Mark. You've not in high school any longer."

"Okay." Clara could feel her face turning shades of red as she swallowed. "How are you?"

"I'm doing fine. You look great, Clara. Are you dining alone?"

"No, I'm meeting someone." *If only I wasn't*, Clara thought.

"Oh, I see. Well, it's nice seeing you. Maybe we can talk later."

Clara held the door open as Mr. Gunner went in. He had aged well: salt and pepper hair, a powerful smile, and still handsome. Of course, he's only 13 years older and she wasn't 15 now, Clara stood outside thinking. She smoothed out her black ankle length dress that was only worn on special occasions, held her head high, and entered.

She tried to look without seeming too anxious. No Tyrone. Clara took a booth in the back, facing the door. Mr. Gunner was seated to her right. She felt his sideways stare as she took her seat.

"Miss, would you like to order?"

Clara was so absorbed in her thoughts that she did not see the waitress approach her.

Without looking at the menu, she ordered. "Just bring me your fudge brownie and a glass of water." Clara smiled and revealed her front gold tooth. She hated her youthful fashion statement, and most times remembered not to smile. "I'm waiting for someone." Clara's head lowered as she offered an apology. The waitress only raised her eyebrows and without missing a smack of her gum, she left.

The chocolate would calmed Clara's nerves, or that's what she told herself. Glancing at her watch, she realized Tyrone was 45 minutes late. Mr. Gunner had finished his meal, but he still lingered, flipping through his paper for the third time. In high school, Mr. Gunner had treated her special, as in normal. She had even been his assistant during her senior year, only 9 years ago. She had school girl's dreams of Mr. Gunner kissing her. She fantasized about him being her first. But he was always the perfect gentleman. They had long serious conversations about her life and her future. He made her feel that life was worth living. The waitress appeared in her dream like a ghost.

"Miss, would you care to order something else while you wait?"

Clara's stomach was rumbling, but her funds were low. When she looked up from her menu, Mr. Gunner stood beside the waitress.

"Why don't you let me buy you dinner, Clara?"

"That's nice of you Mr. er, Mark, but I couldn't."

"Nonsense." Mr. Gunner handed the waitress two $20 bill, "This should take care of it, keep the change."

"Thank you, sir."

Before Clara could object, Mr. Gunner was gone.

The waitress waited.

"I'll just have two cheeseburgers, two large orders of fries, diet coke, and a fudge brownie a la mode with chocolate sauce."

"I'll have your order out shortly."

"And," Clara added, "bring me a salad with French dressing."

The waitress noted the order and looked for more instructions.

"Thanks." Clara dismissed her server.

"What's this?" Clara whispered. She picked up a paper napkin from the end of the table and silently read. "Clara, now that you're older maybe we can finally get to know each other. I always admired your sharp mind, your beauty, and the young lady you were. I would love to see you, if possible." Clara turned the napkin over, "Dinner this weekend at La Petertic? Call me, 242-0876. Anxiously waiting to hear from you. Mark."

Clara couldn't believe that the teacher she had a crush on years ago wanted to take her out on a date.

When Clara's food arrived, she ate, smiling at the thoughts of seeing Mark again. She was finishing her fudge brownie when Tyrone walked in 75 minutes late.

Her smile disappeared.

"Clara, I'm so sorry I'm late." Tyrone talked with his hands, "Oh, you've already eaten? Good. I mean, I'm so late I had to grab something to eat on the way over here. Would you like to go for a ride and talk?" Tyrone's focus seemed directed at her chest.

Clara had forgotten how attractive Tyrone was. And even though he was three years younger, he seemed to like her. But Cleo's words started ringing in her head. She ignored her inner voice. "Okay."

"Good. Ah, you've taken care of the check?" Tyrone smiled.

"It's been paid." Clara wondered if Tyrone arrived late on purpose so he wouldn't have to pay, but his skin reminded her of chocolate and she loved chocolate. Chocolate was calming. Chocolate was her sexual fantasy. Chocolate, but this was a man she reminded herself.

"Good. I mean, you know."

Her fudge bar looked upon her as he revealed his lady-winning smile. Now, that was a smile that could light up a room, Clara thought. If he was a little taller, he would be perfect. And he was showing signs of being a gentleman. Before she could rise, he was by her side pulling out her chair. And she knew it was just a slip of his hand as his hand felt, then squeezed her rear.

He smiled, and pronounced, "Nice."

Clara did not want to know what nice meant because for a second the touch felt good and she did not see a need to object. She was not a good judge of character, but she did give everyone the benefit of the doubt. Tyrone's car seemed too big for his small frame and reminded her of pimp cars from the old Superfly movie. On the way out of the restaurant Tyrone walked ahead of her and did not bother to hold the door open.

"I'm getting ready to have me a good time." She thought she heard him say.

"What did you say?"

"Nothing." Tyrone clicked his door alarm off and entered the driver's seat.

Clara waited for him to open her door.

He rolled his window down and shrieked, "Well, don't just stand there, get in!"

Just get in, Clara yanked the car door open while mumbling under her breath, "Who does he think he is ordering me around like a, a, a dog." Clara found herself saying a bit too loud, still trying to be a lady.

"Get in, I don't have all night, girl." He started the motor.

The tone of Tyrone's voice clicked her back in time when her brother, Jimmy, used to yelled at her. Jimmy always yelled, made fun of her for being fat, and called her "fatso" in front of her few friends. But the last time, Jimmy did not see Daddy standing inside the door. When her brother yelled, Daddy grabbed him by his collar, saying nothing to him. Daddy just raised her face and said, "Baby Girl, don't ever let a boy disrespect you. I only see beauty when I see you. And if a man loves you, he'll see the beauty within and that's what makes a relationship last." Daddy kissed her gently on her cheek and then took Jimmy by the scuff of his neck out of the room.

"What's taking you so long, you stuck or something?! I said, get in." Tyrone's hand patted the steering wheel.

"Tyrone, I think I'm going to pass on tonight. I have a lot to do and it's getting sort of late and besides you were late." She could not believe those words came out of her mouth to her chocolate potential lover, but finally instead of thinking about not having a boyfriend, she began to think about what she wanted and besides his looks, Tyrone was not even close.

"What do you mean, it's getting sort of late!? I come all the way out here to meet you and you tell me you're not going.

Who else do you think will want your fat ass? Let me tell you, no one. I'm all you've got. ******." Tyrone's voice boomed at her as he reached over and slammed the door shut. Still cussing as he drove off.

    Clara tuned out the rest of his hurtful words, but she heard enough to know he only wanted her 44DDDs. She stood on the curb as he sped off. Slowly she walked the two blocks to catch her bus home. Good thing she had saved bus fare. The walk back seemed a little easier and she found herself smiling and singing. After all, Daddy was right, she did not have to be thin before someone would love her. She decided not to call Mr. Gunner, at least, not until tomorrow.

A PAGE FROM MY DIARY

Sometimes there's a pain about being around death. It's not by choice that I'm enfolded in this situation. I have no choice.

There's a certain odor about getting sick. I don't know if it's the fact that you can't care for yourself like when you are healthy or the fact that you stop caring about yourself. Pain has a way of making you less caring.

My descent from normal life began several years ago when I was nineteen and free. It seems like ages ago when I could see, walk, or urinate.

My father had a massive stoke when he was 35. My younger sister Gail and I stood around with big teary eyes watching Daddy's pain ease into nothingness. My older sister, Agnes, ran to the neighbor's, about three mile away, to get help. But we were too far in the country for immediate help, so by the time the paramedics arrived (60 minutes later), Daddy was gone. Mama just sat there rocking with her eyes closed. We knew she was praying for strength. Mama never shed a tear.

Daddy had tended other people's crops, while Mama still went everyday to clean other folks' houses.

At the end of each day Mama would fall on her knees in prayer calling on the Lord to bless her in raising my two sisters and me, while Agnes, Gail, and I sat huddled together in a corner in our own silent prayers.

Being in the country, we always had food and the ladies Mama worked for always gave us second hand clothes. The clothes were baggy and old fashion, but we never thought of complaining. Mama said be thankful for what the Lord has provided.

After graduation from Riverside High School in 1974, the guidance counselor helped me get a job as a secretary and I moved to the big city with my best friend, Lila. I tell you, those were the days. But you know, my Mama thought I was crazy leaving my life in the country where Ms. Mary had said she couldn't wait for me to graduate from high school to come clean her house.

But, I was 19 and finally free and I learned to sin a lot. I figured I deserved the transgressions.

Sometimes my meals consisted of chocolate and potato chips, no more neck bones and collard greens for me. I was free to eat whatever I pleased.

On the weekends, I frequented the nightclubs. I loved the noise, the lights, the music, happy hour food, and those little umbrella mixed drinks that the handsome flirtatious bartenders concocted. I felt I'd died and gone straight to heaven, but Mama swore the city was a living hell.

I spent a lot of my time drinking and going to the bathroom. I always figured I had weak kidneys, everything I drank went straight through me and I drank a lot. Soda was my water and I loved them straight or mixed with rum. Rum was my weekend drink for when I craved to be immoral.

The reason I drank so much was because I developed this incurable thirst since I was twenty. And I never could keep any weight on my bones. But being thin wasn't unusual, I'd been called "Skinny Bell" since birth.

We discovered Club Disco the second night we arrived in Nashville. Lila and I thought we were hot stuff. We put on our shortest and brightest red miniskirts, black fishnet stocking, 3-inch Candi heels, and black tube tops, and we walked the two blocks to Club Disco. My ankles turned east and west with every step I wobbled. But nobody could tell us we were only country.

Being almost six feet tall, I stood out. One guy said I had the body of a model and the face to go with it. I had never had so much fun and attention in my life. The first night there I accumulated a half-dozen phone numbers. We didn't have a phone, so I just told them *I didn't give out my number*. I also met these twins, Rodney and Donny, boy were they cute. You know, being from the country and with my mama, I never had the opportunity to keep the company of anyone of the opposite sex.

Rodney and Donny were college seniors who were stars on Tennessee Union's basketball team. Rodney taught me basketball along with flirting with me and Donny educated me on the finer things in a woman's life. Like how to drive, apply makeup, and stand tall and be proud of my height. In the country we would have said he had a little sugar in his tank, but I thought he was one of the nicest persons I knew. They lived on campus, but spent a lot of time at our place. Unfortunately, I learned how hurtful men could be.

Donny used me.

In order to prove his manhood, he bragged to our friends how he uncorked the Amazon woman. And brothers being brothers, Rodney didn't come to my defense. Instead he lied and claimed they both had had me at the same time. I was still a virgin, but even Lila didn't believe me.

Life went on and I was the bridesmaid in Lila's wedding one year later. I didn't go back to the country though; instead I stayed in the city and learned to make ends meet without a roommate. I still frequented Club Disco, but I learned to return home alone.

When I turned twenty-two my sight started to blur. I managed to overlook everything else, but Lila said I probably had cataracts. I thought that was an old folk's disease. At my age, who has cataracts? No way. However, this scared me enough to finally see Lila's physician, Dr. Hodges.

Being from the country, Mama didn't believe in doctors, only the good Lord. Mama told me to pray and move back to the country where sin was less likely.

But Dr. Hodges told me I could possibly lose my sight - and she read my pain better than Mama. She knew about my extreme thirst, my frequent trips to the bathroom, my nausea and weakness, even about my losing weight and my irritability - Mama told me I was just plain old evil.

Dr. Hodges kindly explained that I had a blood sugar level of 385, which meant I had Type 1 insulin-dependent diabetes. I prayed like a chicken about to get its head cut off for mercy, but pleading didn't seem to help. About a year later I went completely blind.

A PAGE FROM MY DIARY

I have the right to be mad. This cannot happen to me. Why me? I screamed at Dr. Hodges.

I only did half of what she told me to do - I told her I didn't know how to being blind - which was only half true.

I tried to rebel, but ended up hurting myself.

At twenty-eight, I developed End Stage Renal Disease - Kidney Failure - and a year later I lost both my legs.

I cried and cried.

Feeling sorry for myself seemed like the only thing to do. I cried until the pain was mentally gone.

I was only twenty-nine years old when my new address became Southwest Nursing Home. The odor of death smothered me here, lingering in clothing, sheets and the walls themselves. Silences from others surrounded me. The nurses treated me like I was blind, death, and mute. I was just an "old" woman in the nursing home they took care of.

Mama, she refused to come to the city to see me, said God's punishing me for sinning. Mama declined my phone calls and said my sisters were unavailable for a life in the city.

Life in the city hasn't turned out the way I imagined when I was 19.

Now I eat what I'm fed. I sit and listen to the television until I am put in bed. The nurses don't ask, "Bell, are you ready for bed?"

I am no longer free.

They wheel me into dialysis three times a week. I have on my dark glasses and my black shawl covering what used to be my legs. My face remains unpainted. My lips have forgotten how to smile.

The patients greet me by name and the nurses pretend to carry on conversations. Sounds surround me: small talk, televisions, the sweet hums of life giving machines. Here we are a pretend family held together by a common bond of survival.

I force myself to embrace the pain as the two large needles enter the access in my right forearm. Soon, my blood will be cleansed and returned, giving me life, but not freedom, for another 48 hours. Through my four-hour treatments, I think about those jovial "sinning" days.

What would life have been like if I didn't create those memories?

I still talk and think, but most people just see an "old" woman with no legs sitting in a wheel chair with her hair pulled up in a bun with blind folk's glasses covering an expressionless dark face.

But through all my past experiences I have learned I am still a country girl - lifelessly sinning in the city.

JOE'S LIFE

July 4, 1990:
Joe sits at the 3rd and Deaderick bus shelter going nowhere. He has the frayed collar of his over worn brown parka pulled up. His eyes darts right to left in attempts to observe every moving creature through his new found sunglasses, right lens cracked precisely in the center. His possession sits beside him in his brown knapsack. Dirt and hunger are his constant friends.

He stands; his lean frame overwhelms the glass enslavement of the bus stop. Grabbing his possessing, he starts for his new destination of nowhere. Ten years on the streets have taught him to keep moving during the daylight and at night to sometimes seek solace, the good word, and a hot meal at the union mission.

July 4, 2000:
Joe sits on the park bench at Bicentennial Mall going nowhere. His cracked lenses makes seeing difficult and his head hangs downward. The sound of footsteps making an abrupt stop caused Joe to stares, no one, just another nameless Joe. Joe head turns sharply as he senses the approach of a uniformed bicycle cop. No words are spoken, but Joe quickly gathers his

brown tattered backpack. Moving in a circular world. The policeman has peddled on and Joe walks his slow walk. Twenty years on the street, each moment contained in a flicker, no past - no future, just the second. Joe looks around tilting his head upward to see out of his scarred lenses. Peace he finds under an overgrown bush, the warm breeze penetrating his parka, warming his life.

July 4, 2010:

Joe's lifeless body is found icy-cold and stiff under the I-40 Interstate bridge. No ID is found, no name given, no autopsy is performed on the 60 year old. A pauper's grave is given.

SAMATHA'S NIGHT OUT

Let me introduce myself. My name is Samatha, not Sam, but SAMATHA. I am a blue-eyed, full-blooded, wavy-haired, solid white Rex cat, and I'm a house cat and proud of it. And I'll have you know that I have never ever set a dainty paw outside since the day I arrived.

Oh no, there they go again creating nothing but noise. Let me hop up to my customized windowsill, leather padded just for me, and check out the Alley Cats. Let's see, there's Kelly, Bass, Lucky, George, and Little Eva, all strays with no comfy homes. They've been singing together since, let's see, I moved here five years ago and they were out there making noise then. Of course, on a spooky night like tonight with the full moon and the shadows moving, I'd rather be inside, in my safe haven. Miss E, my owner (well, that is, she thinks she's the boss), says it's not safe outside and insist I stay inside.

From my special place on the window ledge, I sit and spy while those Alley Cats are out there chasing all sorts of creatures to eat! I don't have to worry about food; Miss E always has my favorite Jiffy Cat Food ready and available. I like it cold from the refrigerator.

Of course at times I have wondered what it would be like to be free to roam - but then I'd have to worry about fleas and those worrisome big head dogs. I don't care for either. One makes me itch and the other, well, you know how dogs are, they'd chase their own tails if you let them. I don't have time to run and hide for my life - I'm a house cat and proud of it.

There they go again. Little Eva thinks she's so cute with her high pitch voice meowing away. I wish they'd just shut up.

Oh, there's Miss E. What does she have for me tonight - a catnip mouse, yum, yum, my favorite. Where's she going? More food? And she's left the kitchen door open. Should I? Oh, why not. It's a full moon and the Alley Cats are out. Let me just take a peek out the door.

There goes that big ugly part brown, looks like someone tried to paint him white, dog, Gopher. He could stand to lose weight, and what's that smell? At least I don't have to worry about him; I've never seen him go after the Alley Cats. He's more likely to join in and wake the whole neighborhood.

I'll just take one little step outside. Oh, what is this on my manicured paw? It can't be mud. That's right, I forgot it rained today. I can't have this brown mess on my paw, and how did it get on my pure white fur? I can't even sling the stuff off. Well, I guess I'll - oh no, here comes Miss E. Well, I'll get her to clean me up. It's her fault for leaving the door open anyway.

Didn't I tell you that I'm a house cat. I have my customized window ledge all padded so I can look out. Back to my perch and the Alley Cats. At least I finally heard the Alley Cats and know what they really sound like now - a bunch of cats meowing. I could do better. But I'm proud of the fact that I'm a house cat and I can make up my own world. I just wish I had someone to talk to every once in a while during the time that Miss E is at work, out on a date, sleep, watching TV....

Living In The Garden of REALITY
(An Emotional Ride)

welcome to the real world

When Reality comes will you accept it?

VICIOUS CYCLE

You puffed, I breathed
       and the nicotine, tar, and carbon monoxide
       filled my developing lungs.

At first I panicked as my heart raced,
And I mistook moving slower
       as a normal sign my body was relaxing.

However, now I crave your continuous puffs
As you inhale three cigarettes every half-hour

I am your creation,
You breathe life into me
Feed me when I'm hungry and
Let me securely develop within your womb.
      For this,
         I give you my unborn unconditional love

For mainstreaming me into an addict upon my birth,
      I forgive you
For giving me asthma and feeding me

UnBalanced Harmony

second hand smoke,
       I forgive you
Because I too still crave the calming
effects of nicotine

Some gaze at you and wonder how you can
       push me in a stroller with one hand
       and smoke your cancer stick with another.
I, on the other hand, still desire your habit.
You hold me, and I inhale further the scent
       on your breath, the odor in your clothes.
My heart races, my body calms,
I cough and you coo me.

In my short life you have given me
       Nicotine, tar, carbon monoxide,
       Arsenic, ammonia, formaldehyde,
As you've mainstreamed them into
my developing lungs.

As you rush me to the hospital, you don't understand
How my throat swelled, how I've quit breathing,
How you could love me and kill me within one breath.

Now you are again pregnant with my unborn sister
One puff, one breath, one life ending another
When will you stop this vicious cycle and realize that
You are the one that took two innocent lives.

WORDS

What's wrong with your mouth?
So many cuss words coming out of it
I can't find the correct English.
Were those words that your mama taught you,
dialect you picked up from your so called friends,
or words you thought would make
you sound totally jazz,

Well frankly I don't understand your butt baring,
crotch grabbing, can't keep your trousers up,
slaughter of the English language way of life.
Come on, you know, those words won't
make it into the dictionary. Who said, they would?
Didn't I just get my point across
that no one wants to hear all that
stuff spewing from your mouth.

Shut up before that little kid picks up,
looks up, thinking you're cool,
just because he's your little brother.
Why don't you give him a chance to
grow up, keep up, turn the world into
a better place with his individuality.

UnBalanced Harmony

I guess I have to repeat 'cause apparently
you forgot your English language.
I know you hear me, I'm standing up here preaching.
What's wrong with those words
coming out of your mouth?
Every word a cussing, a fussing,
I can't find the meaning or the English,
So I'm just force to quit listening
to the language you're sending out,
Better watch out, or you'll have no audience,
the world will just tune you out
then what are you going to do?

I've had enough, I'm tuning out,
I won't check you later
'cause I can't understand you
interrupting my thoughts to
release foul language in a world that's
messed up thinking that
you've proved them right,
See what I mean?

You could have been an artist,
that next rocket scientist,
anything but what you became -
standing there spewing words and
thinking that you're so "cool"

WORDS

Living on the streets,
don't want to make an honest living,
can't stand to hear the truth -
standing there spewing words…
That no one is listening to.

I AM GROWN

I gravitated to a man with the name of Phil
My mom called him a gang banger
that wasn't worth the time that I dedicated to him.
I was 16 and knew that I was grown
Living in a world that saw me as a kid

I disobeyed my mom and believed the man
That could change me from a kid to a woman
I was grown
living in a world that only saw me as a kid.
I'm grown, how many times do I have to
walk through that door
To prove my man's point of view.

I was out of control and living on the edge
Between being 16 and being of age
I treated my parents as if I didn't care
They only grew louder in the arguments
we entertained.

Didn't I just tell you that, I am grown -
Living in a world that only sees me as a kid
I'm grown, how many times do I have to shout at you

UnBalanced Harmony

My man's got it, you don't have to care.
Two years, one month, and one day later
I'm living in a world where I've lost control,
18, finally put out by the ones that loved me
I'm living with the man who saw me as
A precious little flower he could grow into his own
And product the seed that will carry his name

I don't have to shout that I'm grown,
No one cares what words leave my mouth
Or that I've got a point to prove that I was right
18, definitely living the life I saddled myself with
Hopefully my little girl won't come out addicted

Eighteen,
I should have listed to the ones who tried to tell me
What a waste I'm making of my existence
Two years, one month and one day
they shouted their love
Until one day I was grown,
And they locked their hearts away.

I can't go home, because I've made my bed
with what my mom's calls a gang banger,
He's not, but I am, I just sentenced
my daughter's life to a life long
Addiction to the immoral side of living

16, I should have listened
18, definitely living the life I burdened myself with.
Who cares that I'm grown or
how many times I shout it

I AM GROWN

I'm out in the world, just got high,
and I don't care if I live or die.
16, I should have, but..

I don't have to shout cause I'm grown,
No one cares what words leave my mouth
Or that I've got a point to prove that I was right
Living the life I saddled myself with
Hopefully my little daughter won't come out addicted

UNTITLED FOR A REASON

For a moment I forgot,
Forgot that I was different
Until you spoke up and reminded me

RACIST

You shouted at me for the color of my skin
As I waited for the changing of the light
On the edge of UT campus

Stopped on Green
Rolled down your window
and screamed the N words
to a defenseless 18 year old

RACIST

It's 1976, aren't I supposed to be here?
They say that education is the key
Yet I can't walk without getting yelled at
by some stranger passing by.

200 miles from home
with nowhere to run
I absorb the hurt to keep on going.

RACIST

I turn in my reports before deadlines
I come to work on time
I am the employee who values my job.

Passed over for raises
Promotions going to the incoming
Younger, lighter, seemingly upward mobile

RACIST

It's 2012, I waited for the bus
You stopped on Green
Rolled down you window
And threw yellow liquid on me

15 minutes from home
Retreating within to find my peace
I absorb the hurt to keep on existing.

FREEDOM CAME FROM THE SHADOWY MIST

It was a cold windy night when I first met him
I had just left the one I thought made me purr
He walked right out of the shadows
and stole my heart
That's the reason I gave myself
      For cheating
cheating on the man who makes
      Me purr
On any other day I guess
      I would have lied
But right now,
I'm mesmerized by the figure I want most

He came out of the shadows
Looking like he would own the world
Strutting to a beat only he could hear
Look right through me and stole my heart

Saturday night belongs to couples
And I just lied and cheated on my five year romance
Texted him I just arrived home, but
What else could I do, but follow my heart

UnBalanced Harmony

And cheat with the one
I long to hold in more ways than one

He came out of the shadowy mist
Looking like he own the world
Strutting to a beat heard in his head
Look right through me and snatched my heart

Sunday morning and I'm in church
Praying that my Man and my God forgives me
I'm down on my knees
Trying to get forgiveness for losing my heart
Or is this another lie – cheating on myself
'Cause I've figured out that my man and my heart
Were two separate entities
wanting to divorce our relationship

He came right out of the shadowy mist
Knowing he owned the world
Strutting to a beat heard in his head
Look right at me as he intentionally
seized the heart that
I freely gave him in exchange for finding real freedom

Monday, I'm feeling that a lie set me free
As it became the truth that was buried deep
       down in my soul.
Thanks to the man from the shadowy mist
I am now free to follow the one who stole my soul
By taking my heart and letting me know that

FREEDOM CAME FROM THE SHADOWY MIST

I'm now complete
and free from the one I thought I loved.

He emerged out of the shadowy mist
Knowing he owned the world
Strutting to a beat heard in his head
Looked right at me and intentionally seized my heart

THE EVIL FLEW OUT
(her side)

The evil flew out
and I don't know
I just stood there
as it continued to grow

It became so intoxicating
I tried to escape,
but that brother's life
confused my mind

He had one baby
and then another by me
Two different women
But neither his love

He denied us both
For that steadfast friend
That shoots poison
Throughout his veins

The evil flew out
and he came back to me

UnBalanced Harmony

I couldn't turn my back
on the one I needed

He relaxed my mind
Then tried to sell my baby
But for the sake of my child
I just had to let him go

You know, my little girl
she's a crack baby
But I loved Sophie
until the day she died.

The evil flew out
and I had to catch it
I couldn't turn my back
when he came back to me

Sophie's father tried to love me
but his dedicated seducer
wouldn't let him go,
as he tried to penetrate me.

The more I tried to save him
The deeper down his path I was drawn,
It wouldn't let me negotiate his life
until we both became a part of it.

Now the needle's more my friend then me
I live by the codes that murdered my child

THE EVIL FLEW OUT(HER SIDE)

How could I think that I could heal
the one who suffocated her life?

The evil flew out
and attached itself to me.
I couldn't turn my back
and now there's no more me.

Sophie's death went unanswered
Cause the two killers are now living High
As the evil flies out and
seduces our world.

PAIN OF A FAT KID

They call me names meant to harm,
They've silly little kids that live on my street.
Passing by them every day
as they throw words at me,
Can't you see
I'm the obese little kid living in their world!
Can't tell a lie,
      'cause mirrors don't hide
      just like the words coming from their mouths

They call me names, yeah right sticks and stones,
But my heart breaks just a little every day
Enough to make me stay inside and cry.
Can't you see the cracks you caused –
Look in my eyes; you'll see what you did.

They said my eyes were dead before my heart
Not sure if it was the voices in my head
Or your words wrapped around my heart,
Anyway dead was a kinder way to go,
Thank you for your unkind words

TOUCHED DEATH

I've touched death
    Smelled its presence in the odor of my room
    Considered following for the fear of this unknown
    world

I've been to the edge
    Saw the light beaming in the tunnel
    Gasped for a breath out of the instinctual fear of dying

I've battled to survive
    Bounced back when I should have been disabled
    Denied death the right to take
    me

I'm living a life worth living
    Knowing that my life will be abnormal
    In this perfect people
    world

I'll deal with death's ever-present odor
    To survive one more sweet day
    Because life, not death unknown, is worth the
    Survival

THINKING MAN'S BLUES

Life isn't complicated when you are Three
Life isn't so complicated when you're running at age Three
But let me tell you the Thinking Man's Blues
    hit me when I turned 23.

Love, Hate, Bills can't wait,
I lost my job just today,
I can't take it much longer,
24 ain't far away.
Life takes me down then lifts me up,
Roller Coasters scare the heck out of me,
Can't educate the Thinking Man's Blues

I've got, I've got, I said, I've got
the Thinking Man's Blues
Now can you relate to the measure it takes
Now can you relate to the Thinking Man's Blues

UnBalanced Harmony

Life wasn't so complicated when I was Three
Life wasn't a roller coaster when I turned Three
Just telling you what's coming when you hit twenty-three
The Thinking Man's Blues is going to take control
      and rule your mind.

FINAL ACT

I deleted her from my email today.
It seemed like such a final act.
You see, she died
And I had no choice but to
Terminate her from my files.

However, in my life
She still thrives with every thought
That brings her to mind.

It could be something as simple as
A word or phrase that mentioned,
A smile or stick shift car,
Or the fact that her pictures still
Grace my computer space.

I deleted her from my email today,
But she'll live in my heart forever
Her smile gracing my life
Her wrongful death
Still touch the bare essence of my soul.

For Shirley Ann Akins, (1954-2010)

SELF
LOVED

What a mistake we make
By loving everyone else
And wishing we were someone else.

If I only lost weight,
I'd love myself better –
But with each pound that expires
From my body, I love myself less.

If my thighs were smaller, stomach flatter,
Arms less flabby, feet prettier, face smoother –
I'd be more perfect – able to love me.

Yet we unconditionally love our child
That no one else will
After he blows someone's heart out.

We love our sister,
Who sliced her husband's manhood off
When she learns he's fathered another offspring.

UnBalanced Harmony

We continue to love our mother,
After she throws boiling grits in her husband's face
For the years of being his punching bag.

Our father, remember the time he held you all night
When you were so sick you thought the world would end,
We continue to love him
      even after the fact of beating mom.

We stand by them and continue to love.
We don't question their shape or their reason for insanity
We love insanely those around us.

Yet, we can't love our own insignificant imperfections
And realize we too are a miracle of life
And deserve our own unconditional love.

Take a long look in the mirror and cherish the image
That is yours to love.

MY BOY

It doesn't seem like he was two
      but a moment,
Long enough to say "mama" and steal my heart,
Wobble on unsteady legs and take off to be grown.

It doesn't seem like he was twenty
      but a minute,
Stood up on that stage and
gave his valedictorian speech,
Turned around and kissed his
wife as they began their life.

Doesn't seem like he was forty
      but an hour,
Told me how bad I was managing my life,
Then took my life savings.

Doesn't seem like he was sixty,
      but a day,
As I look down upon my son and smile
Finally forgiving the man he became.

THE HONOR ROLL

Little Billy's on his way from school,
He's so proud; he just made the honor roll.
He can't wait to see his mother's cheerful face,
He's worked so hard just to make her smile brighter.
He knows he's lucky to have Eileen as his mother.

Just as he's about to cross the street,
A car comes from nowhere spitting bullets in the air.
Little Billy darts for cover just a second too late.
He just caught a bullet in the center of his face.

Little Billy laying face down on the corner street,
Caught in cross-fire, he's now laying in darkness.
As the illusive car vanishes down the unbusy street.
No one sees a thing to solve this crime.

On Sunday, there are no smiles on Eileen's face,
She's putting little Billy in the cold hard ground.
Ten years old, so proud of himself,
He just made the honor roll for the first time in his life.

MY LITTLE BROTHER

My mother cries in her sleep.
My little brother's made her weep.
Fifteen, the owner of a jeep,
Parked in an alley down the street.

Quick bucks, easy work, in your face.
Whatever your soul desires
To keep your mind high,
He's the dealer you seek.

School is history,
All he hungers for are dead presidents.
Fifteen, my little brother's
Pulling in thousands a day.

My mother's crying in all her hours,
Fifteen, we buried my little brother.
A junkie's knife ripped through his heart,
Dead presidents drifted covered in his blood.

ANGIE, MY LITTLE GIRL

My little girl's out carrying a gun,
She's out calling herself having fun,
With her intelligence she could have gone far,
But instead she shot a man
        and now she's on the run.

Yesterday I bought her a cabbage patch doll,
I found it tucked away in the closet down the hall,
At fourteen, she should have been watching
        Cinderella,
But instead she put a gun to the head of a policeman.

My little girl called the other day,
She wants to come back
        to play with her cabbage patch doll.
But instead she's using her body for a place to stay.
She knows she'd be dead if she came home today.

The State Police called in their relief,
There's a girl in the morgue they believe is Angie,
In teary eyes I look down at an angelic face,
Thank God that child was not my little girl.

UnBalanced Harmony

Running away from home carrying my gun,
There has to be a reason for what
      my little girl's done,
She only 14, why the hell did she shoot that man?
Angie told me she smoked him in self defense.

My little girl has surely lost her way,
My gun was for protection in this crazy world,
I never thought she would carry my gun to play,
But I know she'd be dead if you came home today.

On the news they described a girl just like Angie
Gunned down in a battle with the State Police.
They called on the phone to deliver the news,
At fourteen, dead is Angie, my little girl.

VIRGIN SEDUCTION

Fourteen and newly outfitted,
She's just a child in her father's eyes.
But to the men of the world,
She's a blooming woman.

Maybe her outfit should have covered more,
Maybe she should have acted more like a child,
But instead she lied and whispered, "eighteen,"
An invitation for sex in his restless eyes.

He wined her and took her to his room,
In his eyes she was a willing victim to his seduction.
But innocent, fourteen, a virgin,
     and loving the attention,
Her eyes didn't open until time became her enemy.

A willing actress in this mixed up world,
She only wanted attention
     like the ladies in the movies.
Instead nine months later she's a mother at fourteen,
Now she's alone,
     no longer a child in her father's eyes.

TOUCHING THE TOP

You know what? I've been there,
touched the top of that corporate ladder,
Life's utmost gift to me.

But you know what? Life took my husband -
he fell asleep after working 20 straight hours -
I admonished him three weeks earlier -
told him he had to work harder,
      "show them you want to be at the top" -
he crossed the medium -
crashed into an oncoming 18 wheeler.
Death didn't smile.

You know his boss was really nice,
said he had put James' name in for a promotion last week
– then he introduced James' replacement
      at my dead husband's funeral.

You know what? I only had $5,000 to bury him with,
we were young - touching the top - no time for death.
Life dealt me a blow that it took weeks, months
      - not really sure if I have - to get over.

UnBalanced Harmony

Took me to the bottom of the ladder,
I'm four months pregnant.
My boss smiles then his eyes examine my stomach.
My ceiling has collapsed.

Look at my picture!
Where does your dream and reality meet?
Shouldn't you know?

JUDGE ME

     You judge me
For the hood on my head
For the kink in my hair
For the attire of my faith
For not looking like you

     Yet you refuse to know
My inner beauty
My zest for life
My Zen set of mind
My admission to Harvard University

     I on the other hand walk with the knowledge
That God has blessed me
That I am at peace
That I do not judge you by your external appearance

     Take a look in the mirror and realize
That the mirror tells no lies to those that listen
For you made a choice to believe as you do and
That my wish is for you to not ever judge me
For my exterior outer shell.

THE JOURNEY

I am from "dirt poor"
    candle lit rooms
    outhouses with newspaper tissue
    Saturday night baths

I am from carrying water from a well
    wringing cloths through a manual washer
    getting a cool drink from a copper dipper
    no inside plumbing

I am from a sea of whiteness
    picking cotton in the heat of summer
    missing school to bring in the crop
    sharecropper's wages

I am from the rural south
    that claimed my mother during a heat stroke
    that sucked the youth from my father
    that made me believe this is my life

I am from slaves
    sharecroppers
    freemen
    dreamers

UnBalanced Harmony

I am from God
    his earth
    his gift
    his dreams

I am from a dream
    to have an easier life
    to be more than satisfied
    to still be happy when life interrupts

SEEING THROUGH ME

I see me - in your eyes.
But your memory survives in the distant past.
It hurts to remember the bond we had –
    the way you smiled, the memories we shared.

Now, I see the fear in your eyes,
    the tautness in your face -
    your unfamiliarity with this life -
    the way you shy away from reality and
    detach yourself from human kind.

You gaze blankly through me as I pretend
    that you try to fight and remember me,
Then one day - I realized your mind gave up.

Your spirit has left, but a shell remains
    that reflects the mirror to your soul
You, who gave birth to me –
    Inspired me to grow,
Has only child like essences now.

I love you –
>	but you left me in the most painful way,

You're still here
>	but you don't claim life or me.

It hurts to see you -
>	be near you,

Knowing you have already faded away.

Dedicated to Mrs. Eva Akins (1932 – 2011)

SOMETIMES THE SILENCE

Sometimes the silence
        Inhales me
Drenches my mind into memories -
Lets me be awake in the darkness.

Sometimes the silence
        Captivates my body
Sending it into unwanted feelings -
Scared to be alone.

Sometimes the silence
        Activates reality
Letting me know that with too much thought
I'd know I'd wish to walk away.

Thanks for taking this journey. I'm looking forward to the next. Please provide feedback at: UnbalancedHarmony@gmail.com or ebuntin3004@gmail.com

ABOUT THE AUTHOR

E. Evans Buntin lives in Tennessee, has a B.S. in Communications from the University of Tennessee, Knoxville, and a Certification in Photography from Nashville State Community College. Involvements includes: photography, travelling, jewelry design, writing, Kids for the Creative Arts (KFTCA), Inc. which brings the Arts to kids 3 – 17, and cats. Evans also produces a line of "suitable for framing" Poetic Art Cards featuring poetry inspired by photos that was taken by the author and artwork provided by Barbara and Leroy Hodges - the Artistic Storytellers.

Made in the USA
Charleston, SC
11 March 2013